hollows

hollows

flash / stories

tommy dean

Alternating Current Press
Boulder, Colorado

Hollows
Tommy Dean
©2022 Alternating Current Press

Alternating Current
Boulder, Colorado
press.alternatingcurrentarts.com

ISBN: 978-1-946580-31-3
First Edition: March 2022

Table of Contents

for Shelby—

Out of all the stories, ours is my favorite.

hollows

Here

We all live poorly here. Use mail-in rebates at the hard-wood store, get drunk at Sammy's on Friday nights, and let our children run around in their underwear through our front yards. They wave flags, swords, and guns, practicing for the coming days when soldier is the only job that comes with benefits.

We all live insecurely here. Guns unlocked and loaded, resting oily beneath dusty bed-ruffles, front doors with deadbolts and chains, evidence of forced entry too cracked to paint over, pharmacy and liquor store heavily gated and watched by paid-by-the-hour security guards turtled in bulletproof vests.

We all live indignantly here. Dig up stop signs and hammer them into the walls above our beds, siphon cable from the trailer-court terminal, pull out surveyor stakes, force our pets to defecate on imaginary property lines, hoist cars onto jacks in our front drives, license plates conspicuously missing.

We all live rashly here. Spending the last of our pay-checks on VFW fish-fry plates, McDonald's Happy Meals, and the spirits of amnesia: vodka, marijuana, and oxy. We roll through town, timing-belts squealing, humming along to 107.3 classic rock, looking anywhere but the fuel gauge, hollering through the stripped-soul ache of being un-known. We race trains and semis, dart through intersections, collecting unacknowledged badges of goddamn luck, leaving rashes of side-panel paint everywhere we go.

We all live permanently here. Football Friday nights, performing-art-center dance recitals, candlelight vigils for missing tweens, bake-sale Saturdays for mission trips and recess equipment, petitions for crosswalks and longer traffic lights. Car crashes, lightning strikes, and messy affairs whisper through the corn-arrowed fields.

We all live ignorantly here. Making references to our ancestors, those who scattered the ashes of cultures they couldn't bring to a caged harmony. Claiming a land that was never promised, that seeps with miasmas of chemical cocktails, evolution feasting on its own tail. We stockpile weapons, hell-bent on protecting our ideals of liberty while riding the twin thoroughbreds of abhorrence and distrust, proclaiming an erosive happiness. This, we say, is the only way to live.

Hollows

We're lying in the middle of a cracked country road, fire-flies blinking a message we're too human to understand. The gravel is hot on my shoulders, the sweat gathering and pasting grit from the tarmac onto my elbows and calves. My chest heaves from chasing you earlier, my throat raw from yelling your name. One look at the way your shoes are planted into the sticky surface of the road, your knees bent toward the sky, and I know this isn't a joke. You're too selfish, too heart-bent on possessing Jody like the Michael Jordan rookie card that you swear your dad bought you, but you've never let me see.

Shoulder to shoulder, you wave the lit end of a ciga-rette too close to my face. I regret daring you to buy them, regret giving you the money, wishing we were back at your trailer instead, arguing over the best way to hold the con-troller of your Super NES.

Your eyes are squeezed tight. I can hear you thinking her name. *Jody. Jody.* And because I love what you love—because I've watched you kiss her, I've watched you hold her hand, play with her hair, listened to you brag about the parts of her body that you swear only you've touched—I love her, too.

So I ask you what we're doing.

"We're dying. Can't you feel it?" your voice oozing with smoke rather than tears.

No, I want to say, but there's a code here, a puzzle that expects something of me, from me, if I want to be your friend. But I feel too alive, too full of promises I've unwittingly made to myself, promises that I'm just starting to see you won't keep.

Your mother lets you stay out all night on weekends while she looks for a new ex-husband. You're sixteen years old, and she considers you adult enough to make your own mistakes. Heartbreak, it seems, is in your blood, passed down through a broken-limbed family tree that shakes its seeds into the wind, sprouting new relatives every fresh wedding season.

Basketballs glancing off the rim, car doors slamming, bike tires whizzing across broken streets, taken over by the whir of crickets. The silence between us gathers like old men at the hardware store. Lately, you've been picking fights or not saying much at all. Telling me I'll never make it in the NBA, that my voice is too off-key to sing along, that the song "I Swear" is really for girls, anyway. Your other friends, the ones with cars and fathers with drug problems, would rather brag about their factory jobs and their access to alcohol. While I'm left trying to master algebra, waiting for my first kiss, shooting free throw after free throw, wondering when you'll come into town.

And as the set of headlights crests the hill, the car steadily downsloping, I look at your clenched eyes and know that this time you might go through with it. All I can think about is the park where you've left your basketball, your house key, your jagged teenage heart. Somehow I know that words won't fix this, that it's my turn for bravery. Lying here has been a waste, that I'm more than this friendship, and that maybe you are, too. But we're too young to see what's on the other side of our lives.

I get to my feet and stand in the light, the high-beams at this angle dominating the road ahead of us, and step over your body. For a second, I'm just another animal, caught in the glare of death's future. Rubber shrieks and sears as the car grinds to a stop three feet in front of my shins. A voice from talk radio muffled in the cab of the car is drowned out by the squelching of windshield wipers flapping across dry glass. The car horn bleats. The driver sinks the passenger-side tires into the weeded edge of the road, stopping alongside us, rolling down her window.

"You kids ... you assholes ... Your mothers ... God in heaven," she sputters.

You wait until the car rolls farther down the road before you start laughing. Giggles that pop out of your throat like carbonation bubbles in a glass of soda. You look up at me, the desperate joy back in your eyes. I reach out my hand, offering to help you, but you don't take it.

"Don't pout, kid," you say. "Nothing wrong with a little show. Am I right?"

You take off hard, almost skipping toward the park, while I watch the taillights of the car enter town, tree leaves shaking overhead. You turn around, walking backward, unafraid of what's in front of you.

"Come on," you say, as if nothing has happened.

I stand there, not quite counting, letting the distance between us add up for as long as it can, thirty, forty yards before I start running.

Always the Alpha

My boy, Tanner, has got himself in some mud up at the school. The principal, Mr. Holler, called me at work, and now I have to go and look that man in the eye and keep my temper. Hours of lost wages, insurance premiums on the rise, and we both know my boy probably did whatever they're accusing him of, but I can't let that man stare me down no more, or my own boy won't respect me at home. Raising boys is like training dogs. You're always the alpha, you never back down, and you demand respect.

When I get to the school, I have to wait for them to talk to me through that little box, peer at me from their camera, wait for the door to click before I can come in, like they don't know I'm coming, like they haven't seen me five times already before Christmas. Tanner is sitting up front, swiping on his iPad, smiling and winking at some girl, like he ain't worried at all. I may have thought that life was a joke, too, when I was his age, but at least I had the decency to keep the punch line to myself. I give him a curt nod, and the little shit laughs. I knows it's something the girl did or said, but if we'd been at home, I would have socked him one right in the mouth the way my daddy did to me. Hell, I'm standing there signing in, giving over my driver's license, smelling the glue and paint from the renovations my tax dollars paid for, and I'm thinking my daddy was right for wailing on me so much.

The principal comes out like he's dressed for a funeral, tie clipped snugly to his sad blue button-down shirt, looking me a little too directly in the eye for our age gap, before shaking my hand firmly, but flatly, asking me and Tanner to come on back.

"Mr. Holler," I say, "I'd like us to talk first before we bring my boy in."

Tanner, standing next to me, his head already inching past mine when he stands straight, says, "As long as I'm home for supper," before sitting back down, resuming his flirting. It's an old family joke that used to be kind of sweet, but the boys—Tanner, especially—have turned it into some kind of mockery. I wave Mr. Holler toward his office.

Inside, the room is wide and airy, the school colors of blue and gold painted on the walls. There's Mr. Holler's diplomas and pictures of his kids. A football helmet from his one season at junior college before his knee got ripped to shreds by a 280-pound linebacker. In a town like ours, people know everything about the teachers and students at the school. We all shop at the same supermarkets, go to the same Applebee's, and hang out at the same lake in the summer.

"Mr. Timothy, I'm at a loss for what we can do about Tanner. This is the second boy he's punched in the last two months. Swears he didn't start it. Says he was sticking up for a girl, that the other boy was calling her names."

Sitting in this padded office chair, it feels so easy to give in. I'm bone tired, though this isn't different from any other working day. "It could be true. The boy sometimes has his reasons. He was gentle once."

Mr. Holler picks up a small football from his desk, grips the seams, his wrist flexing. The way he used to control that ball, the regret arched across his shoulders. We all got burdens we carry like oxen, dragged through the world, circumstance our taskmaster, bringing down its whip when we stumble. "If he was just more like Jake," Mr. Holler says. "Hell, if they all could run like Jake, we could do more for him. Let a few of these indiscretions slide."

"Don't say his name. I thought everybody knew that by now."

Mr. Holler holds up his hands. "I'm sorry. Honestly, I miss the guy. Thought about joining myself, but after the scholarship ..."

The anger my daddy thought he'd beat out of me blooms like moss. I let the moment hang, reminding myself that Mr. Holler is just a kid putting on grown-up clothes. Jake was my oldest. He could hit the seam between tackles before the defense was even set, glancing off shoulder pads and outstretched hands. He led the state in touchdowns his senior year, but he never even got a chance to outrun that IED. The Humvee he was driving took the blast right over the center of the undercarriage. All that metal and bone and skin. We can't even say his goddamn name at home.

"You can punish Tanner," I say. "By God, that's your right. But you know I got to raise a fuss first—otherwise, he'll think I don't care about him. That I'm too weak, that he could do whatever the hell he wants."

"I can take a few threats. Maybe a few swear words. But remember I have to keep order around here, too. Those people out there," he waves the football toward the door. "I need their respect. This job, Mr. Timothy, is a lot harder than I thought. And Tanner isn't making it any easier."

Mr. Holler gets on his phone and has the secretary send my boy in. Tanner walks in, tablet held in his hand, flopping against his thigh. He struts in front of me, taking the seat to my left. I catch a shallow whiff of what I think is Jake's cologne, the kind Jake would use to hide the smell of weed that swamped his room the year before he left for basic. Tanner slouches in the chair, iPad chittering in his lap, some moronic game flashing. I'd break the damn thing if it wouldn't cost me so much to repair it.

I snap the device out of his hands, my anger gearing up like water in a boiler, a few bubbles popping to the surface. Tanner just shrugs his shoulders as if he's untouchable, a smirk forming, waiting to see what he's put in motion. I turn toward the principal, shaking the tablet at him.

"You want your culprit? It's this technology. Fries their damn brains. Makes everything a goddamn video game. Nothing's real. Not pain. Especially not death. So, you want to suspend him, you go right ahead."

"Mr. Timothy, come on, sir. We talked about staying calm. Tanner, here, just needs ..."

I hear that word, *calm*, and I'd like to punch something or someone myself. Calm is the word used by the pretentious, *never had a bad day because I been handed everything my entire life*, but before I can get going, Tanner is standing, shouting. He knocks over the chair in his excitement to stand.

"Nobody here knows a goddamn thing about what I need. Nobody wants to be here except those prissy honors kids and the band freaks. You think I won't punch them again, you're wrong," Tanner says, pacing near the knocked-over chair.

Something is telling me that this is going to get out of control, that the little charade we rehearsed isn't going to happen, that Tanner always was the wild card in this situation, and like usual, I've misread his intentions.

Mr. Holler comes out from around his desk, hands open, palms up, a walking joke from one of those de-escalation videos they even make factory workers watch now. I'd laugh if it wasn't so insulting.

"You best stay behind that desk, *sir*," Tanner sneers,

his fists clenching with the rhythm of his heartbeat.

Everything is speeding up. I'm reminded with a jolt of Tanner at three, the way he'd run around the playground, a look of complete joy on his face, until he eventually smacked into some other kid, the way they'd fall and start crying, the way Tanner would tower over him, always curious at the other kid's pain, never sorry, the way Jake could get him to listen, and later when they were older, Tanner in fourth or fifth grade, the talks the boys'd have in private, before Tanner would apologize, Jake standing there with his hand on his brother's shoulder. We could all use Jake's hand now. Three is an unlucky number—someone always taking the other person's side, an odd man out, and as a father you hated the one left out to be your son.

"Now, Tanner, your father and I were talking before, and we agreed that if you'd just be a bit more like Jake ..." Mr. Holler edges his way around the desk, his belt buckle creaking.

I stand up, and the bones from my ankles to my hips crack and pop. The pain is getting harder to ignore, the way it radiates the brain, little ozone holes in the thin layers of trust, patience, and gentleness that my mother tried to foster while my daddy wasn't looking. Daddy knew I had to have some rough and tumble in me, and boy, had he won.

"Tanner, get ready to run," I say.

"Wait. We agreed. Can we just wait?" Mr. Holler says.

"Do it, Dad," Tanner says, as if he knows what I'm up to.

And maybe he does, maybe he knows exactly when clenching a fist isn't enough, when knuckles have to make contact, erupting like the flame of an acetylene torch, when violence is the quickest answer. Tanner's voice almost stops me, but his pride spurs me forward. Mr. Holler steps back, his youth another reminder of my loss. How badly I want to hit him. Instead, I rake my hands across the edge of his desk, sending the framed pictures crashing to the floor. How often we use glass to protect the things we care about when it's so easily broken. In the confusion, I grab Tanner underneath the shoulder and hustle him toward the door. I'm not sure what it means that I want so quickly to apologize and help Mr. Holler put his family back together, but there's no way to explain my grief.

When we get in the truck, I don't let it warm up. I rip the gear shift into reverse, tires squealing like I'm eighteen again. I know there will be hell to pay for this. You can't knock over a man's pictures of his children and not pay some kind of consequence, but I look over at Tanner, hoping to see the same thrill of adrenaline I feel, that camaraderie, of two guys finally tipped over the edge, his face flush with admiration—but whatever he may have felt fleeing that office is gone, his eyes mutely glaring at the screen, angry or bored, as if nothing abnormal has happened. And I'm left trying to name that feeling when you want to explain to your son that you know why he's doing this, the pain he's avoiding, but this knowledge won't stop either of us from hurting everyone else.

A Thrumming Silence

The day my brother died, I broke into my best friend's house. I skipped school that morning, feigning a stomach ache. I had taken several stool softeners the day before. My mother, a light sleeper, plagued only at night by anxiety that blanketed her like a muslin sheet, assumed that the constant flushing coming from my bathroom toilet was evidence of my flulike symptoms. This ruse wasn't my favorite way to fake sickness, but it was effective, and the symptoms usually wore off by noon. I'd then have the house to myself for four uninterrupted hours.

I must have heard the sirens that day, the entire town erupting in wailing chaos, but we never assume the emergency has anything to do with us. Our minds quickly account for the whereabouts of our family members, ticking off their usual placements, stuck in their settings like characters in a book. My mother was sitting behind her desk, typing numbers, balancing accounts; my father was at the elementary school, teaching science; and my brother was at the high school, tipped back in his chair, math quiz finished quickly, telling jokes that even his teachers laughed at, despite their warnings of detention if he didn't shut up.

I didn't exactly break into Ryan's house. I knew about the hide-a-key, how obviously fake the specked mica rock looked among dull gray stones delivered one spring break when we were eight and were still excited by the loud rush of falling rocks from the bed of a dump truck. Turning the key, I wasn't afraid. There wasn't an alarm or even a dog, but just the thrumming silence of appliances. There was mystery among the familiar. I'd been in the house countless times, but never alone.

The police told us a week later, while we sat on the couch, a May sun streaming in through the window behind us, that witness accounts placed my brother on County Road 350 East, driving at reckless speeds.

"What's a reckless speed to a couple of grannies and an old farmer?" I ask the middle-aged cop, whose gray chest hair I could see through the bulge between the buttons of his uniform shirt.

Officer Fugit shook his head, while Dad escorted me to my room. Dad settled me on my bed, the comforter cold, his hand on my shoulder sweltering. "We're all in pain, Dylan," he said. "Your mother, she can't handle these kind of questions."

"You," I started, but the haunting was already behind his eyes. "Then we shouldn't expect any answers."

Most kids would brag about looking at their best friend's sister's underwear, or drinking the father's liquor, or unearthing the holstered handgun in the mother's unlocked nightstand. But you know where they found me? In Ryan's old playroom, the vintage toys scattered around me—Transformers, Ninja Turtles, He-Man, and G.I. Joe—arranged in an epic battle, a storyline I didn't want to give up, while my mother stood over me, breath ragged as a balloon that's come untied. Her wrists draped across my shoulders, twitching from the mechanical motion of typing.

I held up a Ninja Turtle, the red-masked one, and asked, "Do you remember this?"

We only made it three more months in that town. The rumors were a constant source of embarrassment for my father. Rumors of there being another vehicle, the image of black paint streaked across the bumper of my brother's car that the town sent off to the county dump to recycle and turn into sheet metal riveted to someone's roof. Hypotheses my father couldn't track down, no experiment he could conduct in his lab. My mother lost her nerve for numbers. The steady, plodding pace of a woodpecker at her computer fell silent as she sank into the sentimentality of watching Jimmy Stewart movies over and over, the disability from carpal tunnel obviously an excuse.

And then there was me, suddenly an only child, my brother's voice fading to a single word, "Dude," repeating throughout our new house, his only goddamn word echoing hollowly in the white noise of our abrupt but lasting grief.

A year later, I got a package in the mail. No sender identified, but the address familiar. I opened it cautiously in my room—this new house having only two bedrooms in order to keep the ghosts out—to find a set of Transformers, carefully packed in bubble wrap, the plasticized colors vibrant and unmarked. I placed them on my desk, mechanical arms outstretched, frozen in battle, waiting for someone to notice their struggle.

Wave

You've started talking through the picket fence of your teeth. Drawing me closer with every lisping word. Your breath smells of wilting dandelions, a sugary spike that pokes at the nerve endings in my toes. Your pleas like broken cartilage wrapped in cellophane as you decide if this is the last time you'll leave me.

Say it, I beg, but your nose only whistles the tune we haven't yet placed on the map of your soiled emotions.

I beat at your chest, but the birdcage only rattles, keyless, fragile as plastic fork tines, yet unyielding. Anything unbreakable I find endlessly irritating. Maybe love is one knob turn of agitation away from complete surrender, but that would be too easy for people like us.

I'll say it then, my mouth opening, teeth bridging the gap between object emptiness and the sated timbre of intimacy decoded into language. The fuel needle of my need for you dips, trails, hitches like a hiccup never expressed, because your tears won't stop the goddamn door from slamming shut or the echo that reverberates into space, a place where all I can see is the backlit shadow of your back, bent like those unbreakable combs given away on picture day, boys like you worrying them until they snapped.

You push my head to your chest, but keep walking

until we're outside, night-vision lit, my blood vessels traitorously flowing toward you, an Earthly gravity I regret. I start to yell, but you say that you only want the quiet parts of me. I stomp, I clap, I shout, dancing in the off-rhythm way that follows the earthquakes of your departures.

●

Every month, I take down a new door, leaving them on the curb for the trashman, small offerings to the spirits of unnamed barriers. Cabinet doors pop from their hinges, exposing industrial cleaners and solvents, cups from shuttered restaurants, plates with scratches from your overzealous stabbing of beef and potatoes. The Disney cups bought at garage sales for nickels, while we joked about needing them for the children, the ones this second marriage was supposed to provide, the cartoon faces twisting toward garish impressions of joy you obviously never felt.

When you stand on the porch, your hand pushing through the empty doorway, I think of snorkeling in Jamaica, how you almost drowned, your lungs mistaking water for air, your arms retracting from the fish below, sure you were about to be bitten.

I want to give you a tour of my obsession, but you've always hated mania, and I won't apologize. You've come back, I say, but you're still working out how I can dare to live in a state of unprotected bodily harm. I've gotten rid of the alarm, too, the baseball bat hidden under your side of the bed.

You've come back? This time the question closes to the frequency of a liquid metal being struck by the bow of a violin.

And you wave and you wave, and you ...

An Approximation of Melody

after "Love Street Blues" by Meg Pokrass

I wanted to live on an alley when I grew up. My nose flush against the cool glass, shadows cast over darkened brick, bottles broken, and the shuffle of running feet, the smell of sewage and greasy food wafting into the room, mixing with the *bunanabun* of the *Law & Order* score. My parents wedged into their recliners for the evening, just conscious enough to stop me from escaping. Promises made to ourselves in the night sweat of our own rooms are the lost songs of future geniuses. Even if, in this house, my name is rarely spoken.

The guitar was my first love, and I played until the blood seeped from underneath my fingernails. I strummed the strings on sick days and on weekends when I stayed out too late, my music an approximation of melody. I held the wooden body close, pretended to know what love was, so I could break my own heart, until it beat like the powdery wings of a moth convinced by the safety of the light.

I grew up pill-addled, sucking the chalky residue of Vicodin and Percocet until the tinnitus of phantom pain rattled in my chest. I pawned my guitar, the strings as slick as the bald tires of my boyfriends' cars, each one adding more miles to a body that had long run out of gas. Hold me by the neck, press on the nodules of my spine, and play my harmony until the world sings along. The buskers surround me, the street corner a diagonal from where I'm supposed to be.

I stand in alleys, these not-quite streets that I love, pressing my face against the outside of the glass, looking for a girl like myself, the one I used to be. I rest my hands on empty windowsills, reaching in, my throat catching, slick with notes unsung, breathing away those lost melodies, a ghost of someone's future-past.

A Weight of Risks

The helmet lays in the middle of the snow-plow-scored street, its plastic fractured and bruised like a piece of unripe fruit dropped from an elevation. The silence of an experiment gone wrong, vapors diffusing, pulling away all oxygen.

In the store, two helmets in his hands, hopping from foot to foot, the boy can't decide. One decorated with fluorescent plastic in the fan of a mohawk, the other emblazoned with forest animals, their eyes dewy and dripping. The father on his phone, checking for reviews, safety ratings, an excuse to buy one over the other, weighing the risks as if there is an ounce of truth left on the internet, in the world. Each breath an act of consumption.

Math is a violence, a calculation that hunts even the most prepared. Rules, like bones, are broken every day as the bodies of minor planets collide in the most casual of ways.

A neighbor, unnamed, stands in the shadow of his picture window, playing with the soft, gray hairs on his chin. *He once was, he once was, he once was* repeating in the cylinder of his brain that won't catch, that won't quite fire.

Another helmet, black, dinged from falling fiery beams, rattles against the hook in the locker. Jacket comes off next, but there is something he is forgetting. An anniversary. A childhood friend's birthday. The suck-and-squeeze sounds of the respirator. A home with an empty chair, but a house full of children's laughter. A discordant soundtrack.

Science is insidious. Rules never broken, only discovered. The heart only beats so many times. None of the beats saved or transferred.

The women gather around the base of the porch, a murder of crows, looking for something shiny in the bedrock of neighborly concern. Janice is shushed when she starts with the verses, another questions a song, but the door never opens, no matter how much they knock, feet fretting over the cement, wondering if their duty is fulfilled.

Math and science, the apostles of logic, crackle like the feedback from an untuned guitar strummed by unskilled hands. The father's religion, a weight of risks, circles his neck, his finger scrolling back and forth across the reviews, a yo-yo of second guesses photosynthesizing into the roots of his bewilderment.

A Pondering of Velocity When You're Too Scared to Move

My son stands at the end of the driveway, the tip of his rubber soles balancing in the shadow between roadway and cracked cement. Safety an invisible line I think, I demand, that I can control by saying, "Be careful," but the wind, the universe, the commanding variables of our lives, don't give a fuck, so I count the steps in my mind, brace myself to sprint, holding back my body, because this is independence, this imaginary tether I've created, a facsimile of trust, when why would I ever let him go? The road is too scary, a version of a video game where we don't respawn, we don't rematerialize to make the same mistakes again, where we learn the algorithm of nature, of drivers distracted by another algorithm of beeps and chimes, alerts of someone asking for money, wanting attention, that dammit this driver can't afford to give in this tensed second of my son's life, of my life, a patterned doomsday of coiled, muscled emotion that borders on mania, released in the fragile prayer, of being careful. A haunting from the living, those ten feet that one day I'll never bridge, or jump, or stumble through, or climb, or plow ahead, hands on my knees, a gap yawning.

The Running of Blood

Mandy touches my lips with her finger, pulls at my ear, asks me if she's all I've ever wanted. She told me last week that she didn't mind the car, didn't mind the chances of getting caught with underwear around our ankles. Our first time will be special enough, she said, making sure I knew how to lie to my parents, how to make it look like I cared for once about the football game, how I planned on cheering for the home team. Making sure I asked for money for the ticket, a plate of nachos.

My father had found us sitting on the bottom bleacher of the student section. A wave or a salute, a wink, and he was gone, grease stains dotting the back of his coat as he checked trash cans and picked up litter. Students booed and laughed and cheered around us, while Mandy squeezed my hand. I had a hard time not imagining that each sound was directed at me, my father. I abhorred risks, even the kind that might feel good in the moment. Boys on either side of us pushed us closer together, their shouts hysterical if you didn't care about what was happening on the field.

The lightning flashes, and we press our lips together until the thunder booms. Sitting in the high school parking lot, the football field lights strobe across the sky—permanent stars until someone from the neighborhood behind the stands calls the police, who roughly wake up the principal, who yells breathily into the custodian's phone. My dad will be here any minute, but the thunder gets closer. Mandy tells me that's impossible—that sound is neither far nor near as she moves my hands to her neck, then the space between her thighs. Lightning again, a slice across the breath-caught windows. I pull away from her, and her tongue hangs out there, glides across her teeth, and all I can think about is my dad lumbering out of bed, farting on the bench seat of his old truck, window cracked, the rain spitting on him, forcing him awake as he keeps an eye out for deer.

I open the car door. The dome light is a new beacon. Rain taps on the door handle.

"Shawn, don't."

Her shirt is scrunched like a teeter-totter, one shoulder bare, the other side blanketed. I have an urge to bite the bulb of her skin, to take some of it away on the ridges of my teeth. The rain puddles, mixing with discarded gum wrappers. The smell of mold and bubblegum, and something I can't name. Things without names always scared me, drove me away, and I stumble out of the car, clutching at my unbuttoned jeans.

The rain swarms around the lights. Lightning exposes me as I run past the ticket booth. I want to shout back to Mandy, make her understand that you could want multiple things at once, but something eventually would win, that the deer were always there, cowering, streaking through the dark, instincts rooted deep in their blood, ready to run.

Among Their Skin

Before the cigarettes and sex, a ring of ash surrounded by the lopped-off legs of trees where the children used to meet, swallowing a communion of grape soda. Begging the girls to belch, echoes tipping off chapped, blueberry-swathed lips. We wanted them to be just like us, mosquito bites and busted knuckles, torn-out-jean knees, and sagging pockets. Instead, they hid their bruises in hoodies the pastel colors of Easter flowers. We'd snarl at each other and spit, walking circles around those logs, feral pretensions, while they grasped each other's heels and pulled out long splinters the forest tried to hide among their skin, attempting to leave this place for good.

Come with us, we demanded, we begged, we hedged, but they loped off together, arm in arm, looking back with cruel smiles, knowing at once that we were too afraid to follow. We sat around the fire, the one they started, and whittled sticks to keep our hands busier than our minds, the girls' laughter grown stale and hidden like fairies among the gathering purple dusk.

And what had been our plans, anyway? A kiss, a glimpse of skin around their belt lines, goosebumped and sun dappled, a flick of a thumb across an outie belly button, the brush of cheek across a nose, the touch of soft hair that lingered behind a sea-shelled ear?

Dark. The fire, a sharp corona of light around an eclipse. The dew settled against us. "Fuck this," you said, each word working its way out of your mouth like a bubble you wanted me to pop.

"Give me the knife," I said. "And then just go."

"I need the keys," you said, stomping your foot, and I remembered the way you always acted in preschool. Demanding, never getting.

"I traded them for a kiss." I threw a whittled stick into the fire, watched it catch and light. "I thought it was a joke."

Your knees buckled, and you kicked dirt on the fire. It flared. Your chin quivered. "You'll regret this," you called over your shoulder, your shoes squeaking through the wetted grass.

After, the knife blade—a muted star—I dragged across the lifeline of my palm, blood freed from its tunneling, calling out to whoever was stalking in the mist of the night.

But They'd Never Believe Me

We stood at the water's edge, Lake Michigan frigid in early spring, throwing in pennies from our vacation fund. The Ferris wheel behind us, stationary. A bike without a rider, people spaced out on the boardwalk like lone trees left to wither in the middle of Midwest cornfields. Our marriage was five days old, the culmination of a five-year engagement, consisting of three separate but serious breakups. Our friends casting wary looks behind tight-lipped smiles when we said our vows, the kiss aggressive, our shouts a rally cry as we danced up the aisle and out into the cold. Your uncle's car running, engine exhaust in the corner of each photo.

The carp swarmed, mouths gulping, pennies sliding down their slick throats. You refused to wear a coat, and I won't give you mine. Sacrifices don't come naturally to either of us, and you want to talk about Florida, the sun, beaches as if we ever had a chance to go there. *We could be different people*. The water sloshed against the concrete barrier. How long would we have to stand there before erosion would let us slide right in? Why do I want all the bad things to come from some other cause, refusing to choose? Your father called it a character flaw. The way he made me take a shot in the preacher's office, straightening my tie, his face reddening, rage a guitar string I'd strummed, one that I can still feel reverberating.

It's just the wake. Not everything means something. I lean in to kiss you, but you turn your head, your hair whipping across my face. *Something in my eye.* I don't ask if that means something. I plucked out coins by the fistful, quarters wedged against my knuckles, regret sliding like the shifter in a car when I chucked them into the frothy water. It felt good to make it rain. How it could be anything else for the fish below. To them it meant something.

I could jump in. Say you pushed me. People would believe me. You straddled the metal guardrail, paint coming off on your leggings, skin pebbled from the cold, making the mermaid tattoo on your shoulder three-dimensional—its mouth a pout of disgust.

I wanted to ask what this would mean: The carp closing in on your feet. The lake spray glistening in the strands of your hair. Your back arched backward as your fingers barely stayed attached to the cold metal.

My hands fisted in my pockets, shivering.

The Desire for Predictable Solitude

She holds the jagged, pulpy tooth in her palm; her tongue works the groove left in the tooth's absence. The taste of blood like sucking on pennies, each flick toward the hole a dare. She swallows. The thick glob of blood-infested spit slides down her throat, and her stomach squirms. A second of breathlessness, and she almost forgets not to cry.

Below, her mother is throwing tumblers at the wall. The sharp static of breaking glass followed by her father's calm voice hovers outside her closed bedroom door. Noise hunts her, like the wind or rain or the chill in the air. It threatens to devour every last particle until even the memories of her are scattered like the best of her parents' intentions. She's old enough to know when to avoid her parents, but young enough that she doesn't understand the source of her mother's rage.

At school, screams erupt from the girl's mouth before she has time to think, and she wonders if maybe it's a disease, something handed down from her mother, a jolt of particle passed on at birth.

This is her third dislodged tooth, so she's not scared, knows that she won't be dying today. *Not yet* is a swell of hope, a bird with yawning wings stretching in her chest. Adulthood, she reasons, equals escape, and already she's more grown than she was the day before. Her tongue, too, finds the spiky evidence of budding teeth. At night, shadowed by the blue glow of her iPad, she often looks at mountains, revolving their three-dimensional shapes until she falls asleep, body braced for the first shatter of glass, the sharp words slashing through her inky dreams.

She has special permission to stay in at recess and use the clunky microscope. Her teacher grades papers silently, the swish of photocopies, marking the efficiency of her pen. The girl loves her teacher, loves the silences, her teacher's sighs at the lower-than-expected scores, the way she never fusses over the girl, never prods or jokes. They share a symbiosis, a desire for predictable solitude. The girl squints—the light flooding one eye, and the other closed to the world, is dizzying, but she knows that there are answers here.

Rock, Paper, Scissors (The Bridge, Part 1)

To decide who would jump first, we fell into an old habit of rock-paper-scissors. I won the first game because you always picked rock. I lost the next two in a row because I knew you'd always call my bluff. The bridge shuddered as you stepped onto the rusted metal railing, flakes drifting down to the muddy water below.

"We're going to break our dumbass legs," I said. It couldn't have been more than thirty feet to the bottom, rocks jutting out of the water, its current spilling around the cragged edges.

Legs braced against the railing, your arms and shoulders thrust into the air, sun winking off your earrings. "See you on the other side, Gavin."

I closed my eyes, a camera shutter whirring. The blurry lights of a carnival played behind my eyelids. I counted until I heard the splash.

•

Some days I pretend we never met. No bridge, no pact, no death. Of course, you could never move in next door, your sister never experimenting with meth. There's an alternate history somewhere, a couple of held breaths, and we're entirely different people. But that goddamn bridge is still suspended above that muddy rift of water. The whispers still swirl around me, lurking just outside my earbuds, that Smashmouth song reverberating, synched to repeat. Hopelessness dwells on the other side of this song, a hand thrust out, grasping, continually failing to grip. Polaroids of you that line the headboard of my bed can't smash the image of your hair tangled with sticks and pop-bottle plastic, bled of color as the river mud reigns forever. And I'm left to tell this story, the version changing for each audience: parents, cops, classmates, the fractured selves of this living personality. Maybe I'll always be reaching back, as you sink into that murky river while I rise above into the fog of the future.

A Small Act
of Contrition

Luke volunteered to put together swing sets for single mothers and daycare providers. There used to be a set in his backyard, but now there're only smudges of dirt left by uprooted grass, kicked away by flailing feet. The chains no longer creak but lay tangled among gut-ripped trash bags leaking their spoiled fruit smells in a landfill at the edge of the county.

Amanda Hinkey, a single mother of three, her bangs shyly hiding her eyes, offered him a glass of lemonade. He put in the last bolt, gave the slide a shove, content it would not shift under her children's growing weight. He took the cup, and nodded toward the swings.

"Give it a try, why don't you?"

"Looks sturdy. I like the way you work," Amanda said.

She fit her hips into the seat and kicked her feet, her weight pushing her forward. Nice ankles, slight but strong. He was impressed by her lack of fear. Childlike in front of a stranger. A passing flirtation he wished he could entertain, but it wasn't honorable to Ava.

"They'll just love it," Amanda said, a thrill running through her voice.

Stay focused, he reminded himself. "I'd like to mention something else, if I could?" He dropped a screwdriver into his toolbox. It clattered against some loose bolts and screws. Usually everything had its place and he'd organize the tools before leaving, but this woman made him as nervous as a divorcé on a first date.

She skidded to a stop, her toe catching on the ground. She pitched forward, one hand still gripping the chain, the other reaching out. Instinct got the better of him, and he caught her awkwardly around the shoulders, her bare arms cold below her short sleeves. Her weight carried her through his hands, her body crashing lightly into his chest.

It reminded him of a windchime, the music of collision. The hospital bed stripped, her remaining personal items collected in a paper bag, the metal dragonfly the last to leave that empty space.

"Mister, you've got my attention now," Amanda said, eyes full of life, peeking between the shade of those bangs.

How long since he'd touched the thickness of a woman's hair? "What was I saying?" He hadn't let go, though he knew he should. He'd never had this kind of trouble with the other mothers.

"A story, I think. But I'm still dizzy. Those things are not meant for adults."

Ava's swing set was the first one he'd put together. An unspoken promise that she would recover. That winter, they'd held each other and watched the snow invade the backyard like the suspicious cough that constricted Ava's lungs.

He stepped back, and Amanda moved further into his body.

"You wouldn't mind walking me inside, would you?"

she said, looking up at him. In her eyes, a ring of stardust, a hopscotch path he could take somewhere new. "Then you can tell me all about it."

"I never go inside, if I can help it."

She squeezed his shoulder and stepped backward. "Sure, Luke, I get it. Not the first man that wasn't interested. Thought we had a moment there."

He let her walk away, her strides long, confident, the dizziness gone or never there. He gathered his tools and the excess packaging, stopping in front of the swing. On the ground the subtlest gouge from where her foot had dragged. The first of many, the dirt absorbing the shock, mute, misunderstanding that this was just the beginning. The body functioned the same way, disregarding a few imposter cells until the organs were fully infiltrated.

Luke rounded the corner of the house, and Amanda was standing in front of the glass door, arms spread wide, a starfish, still open to the possibility of love. *It'll wreck you*, he thought, as he closed the truck door and started the engine. That woman had no defenses for this world. He wished he could say the same.

Around the corner and up the street, he stopped for the bus. Children jumped off the steps, the colors of their jackets like a handful of dropped Skittles, their cheeks already reddening from excitement. The last two children to get off were a boy and a girl, eyes blinking from the harsh sunlight. They walked close together, backpacks bouncing with each step. The boy had the same walnut shade of hair as his mother. The girl had the same almond-shaped eyes and the tilt of a puggish nose. The bus rattled past him, blocking his sight of the children. The thought came to him, jagged, like swallowing a pill without water. How easily he could turn around, make up some excuse about leaving a tool. He could wade into the wake of their lives, watch them swing and slide. Shaken by their happiness, buoyed by their mother's impertinent grabbing of his hand. Her whispered promises of what their lives might look like together. Luke gunned the truck, hoping the children would run fast now into the safety of their own home, the surprise of the swing set waiting for them.

Luke coasted to the stop sign. A right turn would take him back to his apartment, where the only presence of children was fixed in pictures that refused to come to life. Take a left, and he could possibly spy those kids coming out their back door and witnessing the miracle of the swing set. A part of him enjoyed the torture. He couldn't tell you why he thought he deserved it, but some feelings couldn't be defined.

He turned left, guiding the truck down the street, looking for the perfect spot. He brought the truck to a halt just past the edge of a white-sided ranch that needed a power wash. No car in the driveway, the windows dark. Two backyards over, the kids, the last two from the bus stop, came ricocheting out the back door. Their mother trailed behind them, wearing a jacket this time. The looseness of their bodies, the way they swung their arms and crowded around the swings, told him that his work was appreciated. They ringed the mother, hugging her hips, before bolting back to the set, throwing themselves into the swings. Luke was gripped by a second of fear that something would go wrong, that a bolt wouldn't hold, but the chains arced, their voices sighing happily with the girl's weight.

He saw it then, how it might have worked out, being invited into their family for some months, maybe even a year. But the family's ability to generate his own happiness would wane like an engine running out of oil until he seized up again, his guilt a stronger agent than any joy they could give him.

He watched them for another minute, the frosted image of his own daughter, Ava, running around the frame, stomping up the stairs, and gliding down the slide, legs tangled at the bottom before awkwardly, like a colt, righting herself so she could do it again.

God's Eye

After supper, we took the kids down the road next to Bryson's Pond to see the body. Picture ran in yesterday's paper of the accident. The kind of thing that makes news in our small town: smashed car with the hood rammed through the interior and door sheared off, its body leaning against the telephone pole like a drunk too afraid to take another step. A couple of officers stood near the trunk, hats in their hands as if it were all new to them. Sure, the car was of interest, but what Hal wanted to see—the kids, too, though I tried to hide the paper from them—was the driver. Some way or another, he'd got himself twisted up above the car in those beams that held the wires. The ones that make the poles kinda look like crosses? Others might call it a T, I guess, but I wonder where their religion lies, you know? The problem, the paper made sure to point out, was that the authorities didn't know how to get the man down.

Even if it weren't proper, a man left hanging like our Lord and Savior, it was a spectacle not to be missed. So we get out there with a haze of daylight left before dusk. The kids are in the back, wondering out loud, curious about the corpse, trying to scare each other. Hal's smoking slowly, really holding the smoke in, while his other hand hangs out the window, tapping some forgotten hymn. I'm chewing on a loose fingernail, even though I know it's not decent and ladylike. We wait our turn in the line of cars, everyone puttering, like we're here to see the Nativity.

When we get to the pole, that body's there just like the picture. Arms outstretched, head cocked to the side, resting on the wire, eyes shut, thank mercy. We sat there for a second, a respectful silence, when little Christine pops up from the back seat, and says, "What did he do, Mama?"

"Do?" I asked.

Bobby laughs from the back seat. "Must have done something awfully naughty to end up like that."

"Son, mind the girls now," Hal says.

"An accident, that's all it was. Right, Hal?" I turn to look each kid in the eye.

"Could be, Marie. But I think the kids might have it right this time."

"I refuse to believe it. Where is your religion, you two? Yours, too, Hal?"

There's a moment of silence, and I think I've finally shamed them when Bobby speaks up.

"Maybe ol' God needed some help getting ol' boy up there into the air?" He sat back with his arms crossed as if that settled it.

"Bobby, don't you talk like that. I won't have it. Hal, tell him. Hal?"

"Oh, leave him alone, Marie. Can't you see we live in a different world now. Carelessness. That's your religion now. No sense, either. No sense at all."

"Well, I refuse to believe it."

We tumbled away from the body, the sun a bright orange marble. God's eye, my father called it. He'd glare at us until we understood that protection and judgment were intertwined.

"Slow down, Hal," I said, looking back through the side mirror. "We don't need any more accidents. You all hear me?"

My family saw that man strung up in those cables as a marvel, something to witness, but reject. They'd soon forget the corpse's message of spectacle, leaving me its lone prophet, afraid that the unusual would become our usual.

Without Permission

The man snapped the picture without permission. Legs coltish, but with the smoothness of an eel. It's her first time in the ocean, though so far only the skin around her knees is wet. The waves seethe at her heels. For this second, the beach is hers, as the frame captures her alone, a single shell stuck in the sand. Fear opens her mouth, and the photographer thinks of a kiss from another girl, on a different beach. In the Midwest, near Lake Michigan, he had tumbled down a dune, showing off. The girl hadn't paused to wipe the grit from his lips. So he continues to search for her spirit, skipping among the waves.

"Wait," the girl in the water says, but the photographer moves farther down the beach. Shock fades to interest. She's come here, spring break, to lose something: virginity, identity, her fear of the world and its plans for her. She desperately wants to live as something more than a shadow. "My brother drowned," she shouts to the sea.

Somewhere, in a magazine, she'll live forever.

When the Waters Came

We didn't move from our living rooms, we didn't turn the channel to the news, we didn't check our phones for the latest warnings, we didn't pack our more precious belongings, we didn't cuss, or rant or rave, we didn't look for boats or flotation devices, we didn't flinch as the electricity surged and boiled around us, we didn't find the flashlights or the baby's pacifiers. We cuddled on the couch, hands and feet intertwined: father, mother, brother, and sister, staring at the screen until the movie blinked off, our own reflections cast back toward us like looking at a self-portrait in a museum exhibit about the end of the world. We refused to believe that this was the end, our fingers greasy with movie-theater-butter popcorn, not even saying the I love yous that were caught in the backs of our throats, afraid to tempt the disasters that hunted outside our front door, but there was something to this inaction, this disbelief, this fucking unwillingness to name our stalking demise. We huddled in the breath of our willful ignorance, waiting for Mom or Dad to give us the sign, but they didn't move. We wriggled up their bodies, perched atop their shoulders, their heads as rigid as statues, while we plotted our own escape, our imaginations stilted by the chill of the swelling water.

Finding Fame on Cautionary Billboards

I'm leaving these cigarettes here because my dad said I can't have them in the house anymore. I used to leave this kind of stuff with you, but now that you're gone, I guess I'll just leave them here. People have been leaving you all kind of shit. Teddy bears, beer bottles, a retainer, and even a flashlight. I guess your parents have been making some kind of list, though your mother tends to cry when she sees the bad stuff. The half a joint left last week made her pretty wacko. Your dad had to carry her away, promising he'd get rid of it. He looked right at me while he was telling her.

Do you think he meant he'd get rid of me, too? I hope not, because no other place feels right anymore. What good is the beach down by the lake if I don't have to worry about you trying to tackle me or take down my shorts in front of those fat chicks that are always there? Kenny's basement ain't any fun, either, now that you can't get us laughing while we're high, doing that gorilla impersonation.

Hannah won't talk to me anymore. Says I remind her

too much of you and her insufferable heartache. I heard she's been riding the backroads with Frankie. Give me a sign if you want me to piss on his car or torch his jacket or something.

So I lied about Hannah. Thought it might make you feel better. We found this place, an abandoned playground, and when she isn't crying, we get drunk and play chicken on the monkey bars. I kissed her the other day, and she pulled my hair, made me promise to get rid of the phone. She said she couldn't handle losing me, too.

I lied to Hannah, as well. I couldn't get rid of the phone. I keep staring at that last text you sent me: "Watch, I'll end up on a billboard." You would, too, I bet, If I showed that to your mom. But nobody wants to be famous like that, even you.

I've decided to keep all your secrets, even though it's hard to look at your mom when she screams. It's even harder when she brings me some of your old stuff, asking me if I want it. I tell her to set them next to your stone. To be honest, I can't keep any of your stuff. It all feels like bad luck. My whole life is starting to feel that way. Like every time I drive into this place, I take on the aura of someone else's shitty decisions. No offense, man, but I'm tired of taking all of this on by myself. You always wondered what would happen if one of us died. Too bad you can't see what this is doing to all of us.

It's been a year, the freaking anniversary. I'm still in town, working at the Citgo on 30. Everyone that comes in for gas keeps asking me if you did it on purpose. I'm so tempted to show everyone that text. Make it official. But it's our last secret. The only thing keeping me alive.

Three Boys
in the Woods

One holding a shotgun. The older boy, Hudson, held the gun across his waist as they sat on tree stumps, debating who would shoot first.

Hudson would have started sixth grade. His accomplice, Curt, held back to try fifth grade again. He was more wild than child and couldn't read. The third boy, River, would never attend school again.

The boys formed an irregular triangle with Hudson holding the topmost point. His intense demand for loyalty paired the other two against each other, so they constantly fought to gain Hudson's favor.

All three lived in poverty, but River's home was a little cleaner. The water from the tap ran without rust, and there were crimson curtains that covered the windows. His father lived at home and mowed the grass. Hudson and Curt both envied and mocked River's normal life.

Curt supplied the shells, bullets made by his uncle's hand. They'd been lying around his garage, easily swiped while taking out the trash. The shotgun, his mother's trophy from the divorce.

Hudson and Curt, playing *Call of Duty* one night, had pointed out how fake it had become. "Don't you wonder what it really looks like?"

"Pretty fucking gross, right?"

"Pussy."

"You could do it?"

"I'd have to be pretty mad."

"Mrs. Garson. She'd be a good one. Blaw. Blaw."

"No, no adults. Never get her in the open. Gotta be a kid. Someone that trusts us."

"River."

"Haha, right?"

River didn't want to feel ashamed of his house, his father, his ability to read. He didn't feel pity for the other two, but he knew that he was different. In fact, Hudson and Curt frightened him. Not in any tangible way, nothing to tell his parents about or the counselor at school, who wouldn't leave him alone. She was always bringing him books, asking him to draw his feelings. Telling him once, "People don't like smart and silent. You might want to talk sometimes."

"I thought we came out here to shoot something," Curt said, eyelids heavy, looking at River.

"I'm not the one holding the gun. Besides, no animals moving around, anyway." River wiped at his nose with the sleeve of his jacket. He had some tissue in his pocket, but the other boys would call him names if he used it.

"Well, at least let me hold it, Hudson," Curt said, extending his arms.

"And watch you shoot your pecker off? I think I'd better go first soon as we find something to pull the trigger at."

"We agreed. You remember, River? Tell him now."

River walked over to Hudson, close enough to smell the gun's oil, Hudson's sweat from holding the heavy weapon. "We said we'd all get a turn."

"Ain't nobody said who got to go first. And I've got it now, so I say that makes me first. Unless you wanna take it from me?"

The other two boys stepped back, their eyes on the rim of the barrel.

The only people River could talk to were Hudson and Curt. Not about books or math. He saved that stuff for himself. But stupid stuff like video games and crummy horror movies. How runover animals were both repulsive and fascinating. The giggle fits they fell into as they dared one another to touch the squashed raccoon. How quiet Hudson had gotten, the way the woods hushed on both sides of the road, Curt's breath so ragged next to River that River wished a car would come screaming up the gravel. Was this the day he stopped wishing altogether?

"Quit screwing around, Hudson, all right? All right?" River waited until Hudson lowered the barrel.

"Wimps, both of you. I was just playing. Bang, bang," Hudson said, falling into an obnoxious laugh.

The last time River'd heard the laugh, Hudson had thrown a lit firecracker at River's feet. There was that feeling in his stomach of heated popcorn kernels right before they split open, but before River could do anything, Curt wrapped his arm around River's shoulder, guiding him toward the woods.

"Let's go find some bottles," Curt said. "Get this show on the road."

If River could be honest, he'd tell them both that he hated the woods, hated the way it made him sweat, the buzz of gnats, the wildness that came uncaged from the loping boys. The subtle gnawing wind of violence that roiled over their small town, inciting desperate choices.

He'd taken to going to the library, hiding from the other boys in the cautious quiet. He loved the clean lines, the way the sun lazed into the windows, no longer a threat.

River stepped on a stick.

Curt yelled, "Snake!" and thunder erupted.

River lay on the ground looking at the cloudless sky, wondering just where the storm had come from.

Swirling Mud Thicker than Smoke (The Bridge, Part 2)

I've run out of places to put my wet clothes on those nights I visit the river. They've done something to the current. Your death has become political. A warning, but also a chance for people to nod solemnly on TV. They've promised no future deaths. Can you imagine making that promise? Fish carcasses litter sand bars rising from the slow trickle of water. Trash wedges against the rocks and broken tree limbs. I stand in the middle of the river, feet bare, shirt tucked into my shorts, the hairs on my knees glistening from stomping puddle to puddle. Silent gliding minnows follow, bewildered by the lack of water.

When you jumped, did you see the bottom, fish darting through swirling mud thicker than smoke? Was there a flicker of thought about possibly surviving, hope for some unnatural intervention? A sinkhole populated by mer-maids or a lost city made from dinosaur bones?

I stand underneath the bridge, marveling at the cracks and warping of the wooden slats. In math class, our teacher tells us that the difference between height and length is merely perspective, an inducement of the imagination, a trick of the eye. But in history, we learn that meaning only comes from documentation, that belief is tangible.

When I ask them to apply these theories to my life, what I mean is your life, but in absentia, because let's face it, you're not here to suffer through the maze of feeling that you've created. How, I wonder, do I document that? They tell me about Hamilton or Pythagoras or Oprah. They tell me about F. D. R. and polio, about world wars and quadrat-ic formulas. They hint at the human genome, the cracked spirals of humanness, like I'm not already alive, not living in the eddies of your choices. These theories, these facts, feel like darts when all I'm asking for is a paddle or maybe a map.

Past Lives

Our four-year-old tells stories, usually unprompted, about his old house, this former life he had before he was with us. He lived on a farm on a country road with John Deere tractors. The deer with the sprig of white tail gathered at the edge of the woods, and he would watch them with his old parents. The ones before.

My wife and I huddle in our bed, elbows and knees connected like the intertwined roots of trees, a mass of skin and bones. We investigate the corners of our room, flinching as the house settles into its midnight dreams.

"These stories can't be real, right?" she asks.

"I'm tempted to contact a forensic artist. The detail is so creepy," I say.

"Did you," she asks, curling her head into my shoulder, "have any previous lives?"

"You think he got it from me? I can't even remember yesterday." I flick off the light, and we lie there in silence, listening to the house contracting around us, waiting for the dreams about farms to take us under for the night.

When I'm alone with my son, scaling the play structure at the park by the lake, seagulls combing the beach for dropped Cheetos, I ask him about this previous life. I'd like to know if these other parents, this ghost father, is a better parent than me.

"Did he buy you ice cream? Did he take you to the park? Did he dry you off with the soft towels after a bath?"

The answers come like heartbeats—no, no, no.

The question I want to ask but can't, a wave lapping in and onto the sand, leaving bits of seaweed, fish scales, and filaments of oil from jet skis and motorboats—Did they love you more?

We Take Our Better Where We Find It

The thump of rock music pulsing from speakers as large as the kitchen cabinets. The sun invading the sheer curtains. The boy's father shaking his mattress, breath already sloppy with the morning's first drink. The stagnant pause, like the rollover of songs on a CD, a signal of misunderstanding. The father's only expectation is that the boy is awake. Maybe the father has ideas of bonding, of working side by side on a renovation project, but he speaks unintelligibly through only music, through these childish attempts to engage with his son.

Layups, free throws, three-pointers, and dribble moves against invisible opponents. A park court with fissured asphalt and broken nets. Airballs and made shots impossible to differentiate, especially when there's rarely a witness, except for on Friday nights when the cars twist their way past the backstop and come to rest, trunks buzzing with bass at the end of the court. The boy stays on his end, twelve years old, a wizard with the ball, pounding the pavement, shot after shot. Drugs are passed around, smoked or snorted, cigarette smoke as prevalent as the smell of barbecues from the neighbors. These vices are never offered to the boy, and his presence is merely tolerated, because he can play, run without getting winded. And though he eyes the girls—these tagalongs with the heavy eyeshadow, the tight shorts, and the crinkled lips—he never engages. Even when they laugh and flutter their thick eyelashes. Butterflies, he reminds himself. Beautiful, transient, enticing, but never to touch.

An adult now, the basketball lies flat in the garage surrounded by last year's dead leaves. His sons sitting in the darkened rooms, playing games on their tablets, their skin chalky and acne-spotted. The butterflies are months away, still enticing, still untouchable.

Temporary Housing

On those nights when our parents fought, we crawled into their closet and closed the door. The muffled sensation of their words hammered at our backs as we dug through the remnants of our parents' past lives. Yearbooks, melted candles, track batons with Sharpied time trials, baby blankets wrinkled with mildew. Love letters and class rings, old football stats. The sheet music for "Somewhere over the Rainbow" that Mom played for the talent competition when she was a junior. Our father said that was how they met, but our mother waved us away, said she couldn't possibly talk about it. There's a lot they won't say to us, forcing us to interpret at night—their barbed words ripping through our minds, fencing off our curiosity. So we huddle together, wrapped in the leathered arms of their letterman jackets. We try to imagine the people they used to be, the people we might become, the people they were afraid to turn into.

Now, my own kids set records, come home smelling of drying sweat, the funk of exhilaration carrying them upstairs. My wife sits at the sewing machine threading patches firmly to the stiff woolen shells of jackets we never earned.

"You missed a stitch," I say, just an excuse to touch a

sleeve, to scratch a nail across dates already too far into a future I couldn't imagine. A place I don't know how to name.

Forty-four years old, and both jackets hang in the single closet of this temporary housing. I'm too often jolted into the imagining—a dark night, sharp curve, the glow of a cell-phone screen, the refracted words of a text bobbing across your eyes like a buoy at the end of a pier. If you came in the door tonight, yelling my name, you'd find me in the closet, leather arms wrapped around my shoulders, phone cradled against my ear, breathing collectively with my siblings, listening to our mother's song, asking where did we go wrong.

Flames,
Licking, Impossibly

I stood outside this little shop of decorative mirrors, and I watched the crowd seethe and twist like a basketful of riled snakes. *Revolution*, they insisted while smashing bank windows and setting cars on fire. Gas tanks rarely full, now explosive. What would it take for us all to combust, to flame out, swirl into wisps of smoke creating vertical rivers of unmet demands of potential energy?

My mama said I was too small to participate, that my place was at home, hiding underneath the bed. The sirens called me out, the twittering pipe of a snake charmer, leading me into the chaos of elbows and hips marching down the throat of the city. The tongue of marchers swished me from side to side like an attempt to dislodge a popcorn kernel. Men ignored me like a father who owes too much child support; the women called me child, shooing me toward the alleys and side streets murky with darkness. *You should not be here. We will fight for you.*

In front of the mirrors, the people loomed like

buildings, their faces made of steel and glass, a maw of broken teeth. They surged forward, guided like waves onto a beach, colliding with the barrier of police. A teenage girl fell in the street, and I thought of those other buildings, fogged with smoke, flames impossibly licking at the sky. So, I ran to her, weaving between the heavy steps of work boots and the whispering soles of ground-down tennis shoes. I offered my hand, my back a shield, but she just shook her head, so I stood there in the wake of this revolution, wondering who would see me and what they would think, a picture of children in the sea of political unrest, where we were all just the debris tossed upon violent waves.

We're Trying to Tell You

My dad says he's tired of turning off the lights, that he works too hard to be nickel-and-dimed by the energy company, that if we're only going to move from room to room, eyes pivoting from screen to screen, then the least we could do is flip a switch every once in a while—that is, if we want to continue to have Wi-Fi and HBO, and Xbox Live, and soda, and pizza every Friday night. A little respect is all he's asking for. But of course we ignore him—it's either that or tell him to go fuck himself. In our last kids-only family meeting, however, Jett said we had to keep Dad on the even keel, that if we wanted to avoid counseling and a barrage of new medications, if we wanted to avoid the screaming and the threats, we'd better lay low—that turning up the volume on our iPads was a better way to go about ignoring Dad's new crisis. Besides, it kept Mom from getting her headaches, from binge watching those trashy housewives shows.

I'm not the one who usually gives a shit about parental

issues. We save that crown for Hope, a middle child if there ever was one, and her constant attempts to get someone to notice her. You know those stupid challenges: Tide PODS, salt, Momo, planking, or whatever, she's done them all. Every six months she goes to the hospital puking or gasping or screaming, and me and Jett just shake our heads. We'd like to help Hope, but she thinks we're the problem. It does not help that she hates music, that her life is more dramatic than any show on TV, that she'd rather sit in her room cutting off the bottom inches of her new miniskirts.

But tonight, when I walk in the door, late because I skipped the bus to try skateboarding at the library, Dad is standing in the kitchen, his forehead greased with sweat from some chore we've been refusing to do, flipping the light switch on and off. Mom's nowhere in sight, and she's the only one who can calm him down when he's freaking out. Jett and Hope are sitting at the table, the one that still has stains on it from our paint and marker days, the one our mother would love to replace but Dad refuses to throw out. Mom's always begging for new furniture, says it would finally make her feel at home, even though we've lived in this house since I was a baby. Jett and Hope don't have their headphones on or their phones out, and it feels like I'm walking into a courtroom. Jett doesn't even smile when I say, "What's up, Pops?"

"Have a seat, Chance. There's something we need to get straight," Dad says, the lights flashing on and off.

"Can't we skip the lecture. I mean, we know it all by heart. Work too hard. Bills. Lazy. Shape up or ship out," I say, turning toward my siblings, but either Jett's really high or he's been crying, and Hope is never this quiet. I can usually count on her to distract Dad long enough for me to make it to my room unnoticed. And where is Mom?

"You don't want to sit, that's fine. But you'll goddamn hear me for once." Dad leaves the light switched off, puts his hand out as if to grab my shoulder, but I'm already ducking away toward the refrigerator, pulling it open hard enough to make the condiments jangle in their glass jars.

"Did you run this little speech past Mom?" I rummage around until I find a Lunchables and a Pepsi, hoping Hope hasn't eaten all the fruit snacks.

"Your mother," Dad says.

I close the fridge door, hands full, and now Dad's crying, too, and god, as if this wasn't the worst play I'd ever seen. "What about her? Did she finally go crazy?"

Dad crumples into the chair, the wooden back popping.

"Chance, we're trying to tell you," Hope says. She hovers next to Dad, her hand resting on the chair back. Her fingernail polish is dark purple but chipping.

"I thought we agreed to leave the old man alone," I say to Jett.

"He's in charge now," Jett says, wiping at his nose with his sleeve like a toddler with a nasty cold.

I pop open the Pepsi because I don't know what to say. I'm tempted to run out of the room, but even if I don't like them much, they're my family, and however this bad news turns out, I need to hear it.

"She freaking left, man. Like, packed up all her clothes and jewelry, left a note with an address, kind of never coming back—left," Jett says. There's something about his eyes, the shape of them that reminds me of Mom, and I step toward him because I want to punch away that resemblance. He doesn't even flinch, and our dad is reaching out, and we're holding hands, and I don't let go, because it's better than him flipping the lights, a code that might have said *I love you*, but our mom must have misunderstood, must have heard *I won't, I won't, I won't—change.*

Carrying the Weight

Eric, a middle-school history teacher, stood in line at the supermarket, ducking his head to go unnoticed. Though he only had a few items, he hated the self-checkout machines, afraid he'd make a mistake or the price wouldn't ring up right. Some of the employees were his former students: conversations like scripts from bad commercials he could not suffer through again. So, he waited in the express lane, the opening like a World War I trench, flanked by aging candy bars and other impulse-buy items, which had become surprisingly hi-tech in recent years. Cell phone chargers, wireless speakers, and earbuds colored like cotton candy. All of this technology, and the older lady in front of him was paying with a check. Her fingers fumbled through the writing process. The checker, a forty-something with crimson hair, distractedly spun the carousel of plastic bags awaiting their journey to a landfill.

Eric, sweat ebbing from his hairline and drying on his face, was jittery from his workout, an edge of adrenaline fizzling underneath his skin. He reminded himself to chill. A phrase he employed against the rage of ADHD that filled his classroom.

The older lady's check was approved, and Eric inched his cart up, jockeying for more space. The line behind him was occupied by a young boy and a gentleman surely too old to be the father, but too young to be the grandparent. Family demographics were so strange these days that Eric often felt lost in the world, unsure of who belonged together.

The boy was whining, his voice growing more desperate—louder—as he picked up each package of candy. The man, dressed in a soiled Carhartt jacket, wearing out-of-date wire-rimmed glasses, kept telling the boy no. His voice throttled out a warning the boy didn't want to hear.

As Eric reached for his membership card, the checker greeted him with a sigh, swiped the card across the scanner, then handed it back without saying hello. Eric avoided saying any more than he had to, afraid to give the woman a chance to launch into her worries of the day. People, Eric had noticed, were becoming more prone to oversharing.

His steaks, a baking potato, sadly wrapped in plastic for quick cooking in the microwave, a bunch of bananas, and a six-pack of toilet paper went through the scanner without comment.

"You never get me anything," the boy in line said, his body jerking like a windsock, wiggling closer to Eric.

The father growled. Fierce and foreboding. He pulled the kid away from the rack, PayDays raining from the boy's hands, clattering to the ground at Eric's feet. The boy stomped, kicking one bar under the rack, knocking another against Eric's shoe. Eric reached down to pick up the Pay-Day, meeting the boy's gaze: eyes of rage and tired with frustration, a twinkle of manipulation that harbors itself deep inside certain children's souls, bubbling up, silently begging for an accomplice.

It was clearly one of those classic don't-get-involved moments. One you'd tell your wife about, laughing at how badly another parent handled the situation. *I mean, he actually growled*, Eric would have said, his wife swatting his arm, chortling, her voice ringing like a cleft bell, until tears emerged. If they were still together—but these conversations were no longer in his life. Hadn't been for years. His own children no longer begged him for candy or much of anything now that they had their own families to worry about.

His last item on the belt (a box of Cheez-Its) he'd eat while drinking a few beers tonight as the sun set. He'd finally given up pretending he'd cook the steaks that moved smoothly each week from the checker's hands and into the waiting plastic bag.

The checker pointed to Eric's hand, asking him, "Want that, too?"

The boy was quiet, arms crossed. His father's large hands pressed over the boy's shoulders. We put so much weight on them—kids—with our words and hands, forcing them to drag a loaded sled into adulthood.

"Might as well," Eric said, handing over the candy. A final beep, and then the checker was reading off his total. Eric put his debit card into the reader and pushed the little green button.

Arriving

He pulled into the driveway and saw Ruth sitting on the front porch steps, bundled in her parka, wool mittens, and a black stocking cap. Her arms cradling her legs, she looked like a child waiting for her father to arrive home from work. In the headlights, her eyes were radiant in the brisk chill of the coming dark. He cut the engine and scrambled out of the car. The snow crunched under his feet.

He placed his briefcase on the step beside her and sat down, careful to avoid the melting snow. She leaned her body into his, and he put his arm around her. He couldn't feel the heat of her through the heavy fabric of their coats.

"You missed them. They built snowmen."

In the neighbor's front yard sat four snowmen in different shapes and sizes, each, he imagined, made to represent a member of the family. He concentrated on their features and was mildly shocked by the placement of the eyes, mouth, and nose on the smallest one. It looked like an expressionist painting, with everything slanted to one side. If it were his child's, he would have waited until the boy went inside and then corrected it.

"How long have you been out here?"

"An hour, who knows. After the appointment … I don't know."

He was amazed at the airy silence; shadows brave against the dying sunlight bounded around corners as the streetlights popped on. The search for the perfect excuse stirred in his hands and legs, keeping him warm. The little snowman made him anxious, as though its imperfections would somehow ruin his explanation.

"I was sitting here trying to think of a way to hide it from you, but when those children came plowing out that door, I lost it."

He stood then and looked down at his wife, her face veiled in his shadow, her eyes liquid, cheeks windburned and chapped, and then she shivered. "Ruth, I'm sorry. The couple showed up late, and there was all that snow melting on the hardwood floors. I couldn't just leave it that way."

"It doesn't matter. Forget it, okay?" She stood, too, wrapping her arms around his waist. She looked up at him. A strand of hair came out from underneath her hat, resting over her eye. "Dr. Lesko went over our test results again, and there's just too many of those things. God, I can't even say the word."

"Cysts?" he asked, his voice sounding too loud in the muted darkness.

"Yes. God, cysts." She dropped her arms from around his waist and crossed them over her chest.

"If there was something I could do …"

"So you're off the hook," she said.

"But I'm still your guy, right?"

"Oh, hell, you know what I'd love?" she said. "I'd love to wake up tomorrow and look out the window and see them gone."

In front of him, a vista of white decorated the neighborhood like a baker's frosting: cars, roofs, yards, and scaly tree branches doused in confectioners' sugar. Above and below him, sky and ground shimmered like tiny pen lights. "I could do that, I could."

"God, I'm so … so utterly … Don't I deserve to be angry?"

"I think it's only natural," he said. "What if we had something else to concentrate on?"

"Not you, too. Don't patronize me, not now."

Staring down the street, he thought of all the parents putting their children to bed, giving them a quick kiss on the forehead, before the parents headed off to their own rooms, where they'd cuddle together under the heavy covers. They'd fall asleep knowing their children were safe and warm, happy to have another day in a happy life. Well, that pissed him off because he, too, wanted to know just who had decided that they couldn't have the same damn things.

"I can't look at them anymore. It's like they're watching me," she said.

"Go, then." He softened his voice. "I'm right behind you. I just need to get something from the car."

She sighed, her breath turning to fog, then dissipating into the night. "Take your time. I guess that's all we have left."

She clomped her shoes on the porch, creating watery footprints. After she closed the door, he watched her walk farther into the house, coat and shoes still on. The water from her shoes would hide in the carpet and later he would step in it, soaking his socks and freezing his toes, his circulation too slow to keep his feet warm. Every winter they went through the same thing: he'd ask her not to wear her shoes past the kitchen, and she would claim to forget. Ten years of marriage, and nothing had changed.

He dashed across the street, almost slipping but regaining his footing, and stood in front of the two smaller snowmen. He raised his foot and kicked at the base of the taller one. A chunk of snow collapsed to the ground, and the midsection shuddered and canted to the left. He then punched and pawed at the baby until his hands were cold, red, and raw with the crust of melting snow. A carrot, broken in half, lay at his feet near the squished Oreo that used to be its eye. He turned his back on the mess and walked away, knowing that his footprints would harden overnight, and that tomorrow, his neighbor would find the smashed snowmen and wonder who had invaded and caused such destruction in their happy lives.

Ruthlessly, Denying

Veronica stood inside the closet and pushed the hangers back and forth, the rattle of plastic, a distraction from the horror film that privately played through her mind. Cady's death, a shock like being struck by lightning—a thing so bizarre as to be laughable had it happened in a movie. *Fuck* was the only word to describe her grief, and until now she was too afraid to say it out loud. She stepped out of the closet, hands on her hips, and said, "Just what the fuck am I supposed to wear?"

He cringed, and the beer tipped off his stomach and onto the bed, the liquid sloshing out of the can. It puddled and soaked into the sheet and then into the mattress. Scooping up the can, he jumped out of the bed. No sounds, but the heavy suck of breath through his nose and then out as he cried. She knew he was just as devastated as she was, probably more so, but she wanted to wreck him, the way she felt every time she saw one of those Rockwell paintings. She walked around the edge of the bed and put her hand on his shoulder, and he shuddered like a semi braking hard on a short yellow light.

"Don't. Okay?" he said. "Just don't."

She didn't know if he meant the cussing or the touching. If she had a can-opener, she'd crank open his skull and wait for his thoughts to spill out on the floor between them. "Russ, I'll take care of it. Everything," she said, dropping her hand to the edge of the sheet.

"Leave it. I'll just sleep on the couch. I can't take any comfort in it, anyway. I deserve a whole lot worse."

Veronica hated the way he could take the air out of her anger, popping the balloon rising in her chest, by saying the things she wanted to say. It left her unsettled, unsure of what to say next, especially when she wasn't sure she was done trying to hurt him. Their marriage didn't used to thrive on hurt, but the pain from Cady's death was like an autoimmune disease, targeting her very cells, prodding them until they were about to burst.

"Give me five minutes, and you can come back and lie down. Half of it's your bed, too."

"Forget it," he said. "I'll go check on the truck." He sucked in his snot like a child, the sound stopping them both, each of them thinking of Cady, the things she would no longer do.

Veronica shook out the new sheet, the fabric billowing between them. When it fell twisted onto the bed, Russ was standing in the doorway, hands braced against the wood, his back to her, speaking into the other room.

"I've seen people do this in the movies," he said. "The man who is so overcome he can't make it out of the room. I thought it was so fake, so Hollywood, but I get it now. Like those runners who crawl across the finish line. I never understood that level of exhaustion."

She can't touch him, can't punch him, can't scream; she promised herself that she was done with that. She bent over the bed, the smell of beer too close to her face for comfort, but she fussed with the corner, pulling it tight around the end of the mattress until he left, his steps heavy on the doublewide's floor. She refused to follow him, thinking that they both deserved their own spaces, not knowing if this, more than the act of the death itself, would break them.

When she got to the last corner, the sheet bunched in her hand, refusing to move forward. She'd put the sheet on the wrong way, and she would have to start over. She rarely got it right on the first try, but those small domestic hang-ups found the dark center of her grief and anger, each one another indignity. She ripped the sheet off and flipped it into the air, settling it correctly this time, the fabric floating like a single tawny cloud, so round, like Cady's cheeks. This was the difference for a mother—every goddamn thing reminded you of your children. Physical pictures were for the other family members; mothers had images and snippets of videos that ran through their consciousness, waiting in the background of their minds like land-mines, popping up and exploding at the most unreasonable times without the slightest provocation.

"Fuck," she said, the sheet falling to the bed, wrinkled and lifeless. They wouldn't break, she thought. They'd weather together, beat to hell by their grief, where they'd find shelter in each other, or they'd erode slowly like islands awaiting the water rushing over their shores until the only evidence of their marriage existed in pictures—like long-forgotten maps of forgotten cities.

Just the Father

Shane stands in the living room of his new apartment and tries to think of a way to keep his wife from leaving him again. It happens every Friday when Rachel drops off their daughter, Kya, and it occurs again when Rachel picks her up on Sunday afternoon.

Today, Rachel arrives early, walking in before he could get to the door. A feeling of hope starts low in his gut and swells upward like a released bird, but her face is flushed with anger before he even says hello, because, she reminds him, they are late for a birthday party, and didn't he also remember her explicitly asking him to have Kya ready, and where was the dress and her backpack with all of her supplies? And though he's sure she never told him about any parties, he helps her gather Kya's stuff and pleads with the little girl to "Let Mommy do your hair." Adding words like pretty, princess, and beautiful, though he wants to tell her that she's all of these things already and putting her hair in a ponytail won't change that, but he's just the father now. The man that is fun to be with on the weekends. A respite that he's afraid she'll soon hate.

"Gimme juice," Kya says, her whole body shaking. They're seconds from a complete meltdown.

"This is really eating up my time," Rachel says. "I don't

know why you can't come to the house."

"This is a part of our agreement, remember?"

"Could you just get her the juice?"

He won't tell her that going to the old house would be too painful. That he's afraid of running into one of their old neighbors. That if he walked through that door, he did not think he could leave on his own. So, instead he makes Rachel come here, to his sparsely furnished apartment, hoping that she'll see that he has no intention of starting a new life and invite him back home. Six months have passed, and he's still coming up with excuses to make her stay.

Now, Kya cries from the living room, while he rummages through a kitchen cabinet looking for the new sippy cups he bought last week for Kya's visit. The search for a cup is a nice distraction, a chance for him to come up with a plan. A lawyer for a nonprofit company, he has a lot of time at work to run scenarios through his mind, but nothing seems to work. Over the last several weekends, he's already offered Rachel coffee, a three-course dinner, and a kids' movie they could watch together as a family. All offers turned down. He was running out of ideas. Even having her in the other room was better than watching the door shut as they left him—Shane always hovering behind the blinds, waiting until her car pulled away before he returned to the task of cleaning the piles of Kya's crayons and stickers, "letters to make you happy while I'm with Mommy."

He pulls open cabinet after cabinet, afraid he's used the last clean cup already. Three cups sit next to the sink. A skim of juice or milk rests at various levels, souring in the room temperature, because he keeps forgetting to put them back in the fridge after Kya loses interest. All weekend his daughter has flitted from toys to crayons to animated shows he can't name, becoming bored in an instant, and causing him no small amount of irritation over her unwillingness to attend to one task. He felt uneasy in her presence, as if she were waiting for him to fail, so she could tell her mother. Sure, he loves Kya, but it was easier when all three of them were together. Rachel held them all together.

Shane finds the cup sitting next to the rest of his ragtag collection of glasses, which are mostly take-out pizza cups and the coffee mugs he's grudgingly taken away from conferences. He pulls it out and pops off the lid. It's one of those plastic cups that the advertising promises you can throw away, and maybe he will once he's moved back home. In the few steps from the cabinet to the fridge, he prays that he has some juice left. He opens the fridge, and the bottle is sitting there among the scant items he keeps stocked. Some pickles, a bottle of ketchup, and a package of hot dogs lay in half-consumed states on the various shelves. He has never learned to cook, so he usually waits at the office until he's hungry, then picks up fast food on the way home to his empty apartment.

"Don't forget to add the water," his wife yells from the other room, though her speech is garbled as if she's talking with a hair tie or the comb in her mouth.

He pours the juice directly into the cup, refusing to add the water. He's made all of Kya's drinks this way since she arrived Friday night. It's a small thing, but he likes this kind of cheating—the kind that doesn't really hurt anyone, but gives him a small rush, anyway.

"Hurry, Daddy," his daughter shouts, followed by "Ouch, Mommy."

"Hold still, Kya. I'm almost done."

Pouring the juice, he understands now, he's become a bystander, a father who is allowed to watch, but never expected to intervene. His wife, whether by design or not, is pulling away from him. Or maybe he is doing it to himself. All that time, he was stuck in his routine, hustling to get to work, thinking that this finally is what fathers did, when he should have been paying more attention.

He pushes down hard on the lid, because already this weekend Kya spilled her cup all over her clothes and cried until he got her into the bath. He gets most of the lid secure, but the section in the front doesn't want to close. If he wasn't paying attention before, he is now. Here's his chance to get his wife to stay. He hates using his daughter this way, but he leaves the cup as it is and walks into the other room, holding his breath and waiting for Kya to scream.

Baby, Alone

There is a baby, alone, in a car across the parking lot aisle. I can't quite make out its face or its gender. I concentrate on the flash of red fabric, which I assume is its arm clothed in a shimmering coat. It's much too cold for a baby to be alone in a car. I tell myself this, as though there are a set of perfect conditions where a mother or father might be allowed to leave their child, almost an infant from the look of its tiny fingers, in a parked car in the parking lot of one of the largest shopping centers in town.

My own car is running, the slight mumble of my husband's talk-radio station turned down low, competing with the flutter of the engine. We're here for a pregnancy test, an argument he won, because, like I told him, I'm familiar enough with my own body to know if I were pregnant or not. He kept pointing to the logic, a counting of days since my last period as if that were enough to convince my uterus not to bleed.

Right or wrong, I agreed to go with him to the store but told him that was as far as I would go. The rest was up to him. "It's your time dime," I told him.

He gave me a look. He hated when I fell into the pulpy sayings of my father. When you've been married seven years, sometimes a look is all you need to communicate.

"Leave the keys," I said as he unbuckled too quickly, the metal striking the window. The sound stilled the air.

"Can I get you anything else?" he asked.

I was tempted to ask for a bottle of wine. We'd need it after the failed test, but I didn't want to push the issue. He hated when I was right as much as I hated it when it snowed. It looked like we'd both end up losers tonight.

When I didn't answer, he leaned in and kissed me on the cheek, a cute gesture, like we were still dating, and I couldn't help but smile. He opened the door, and the cab filled with the smell of fried food. The outdated air freshener hanging from the rearview mirror danced in the cold breeze.

I watched him walk away, and as soon as I thought he was out of earshot, I started the car and prayed we had enough gas to keep it running. I was too afraid to look at the gas gauge. There were a lot of things I was afraid to look at these days.

I sat in the heat, watching the people brace themselves against the cold. I spent several minutes watching a woman in a thin jacket with a short dress, legs covered in tights, walk backward. She got me thinking about my husband again. I wondered if that's how he saw me, a frail and huddled bird? The woman shrank between two SUVs, the largest one's lights flashing as she unlocked the vehicle. That's when I saw the tiny movements from the car across the aisle.

At first, I wasn't sure I'd seen anything, especially with the sun setting over the ridge of the supermarket roof and the shadows rolling in like fog. But there it was again, like the flutter of a hummingbird's wing. I turned down the heat and then the radio as if I could also hear the movement from the car. Another car rattled down the lane and passed between us, blocking my vision. I craned my neck to the left and then to the right, my cheek resting against the window. As far as I could tell, there was no one else in that car, certainly no adults in the front seats, and no other children in the back.

Minutes passed in that state of anxiety that grips you when you know you need to make a choice. I played with the heater, turning it up and down, focusing my thoughts on the rush of the air from the vents. I punched at the radio buttons until my neck itched. There was that feeling you get when you wish you could just walk away into another life. The lives you've allowed other people to lead for you.

When I get to the car, I expect to see the baby crying, but it quietly looks at me, and I wonder what it's trying to tell me. The baby is a boy, with a shock of light-brown hair spilling out of a slanting toboggan hat. He looks away from me, and I tap on the glass. He smiles, flails his arms, and gurgles something at me in baby-speak. The wind is at my back, roiling over my legs, chilling the backs of my knees. I try the handle, wondering why it's taken me so long to do it in the first place. The handle clicks, but the door doesn't open.

"Small miracles," I whisper toward the glass, and it fogs. The baby wags his head, looking around the condensation as if I'm something worth seeing. People drift by, pushing their rattling shopping carts. The wind picks up their voices and the rippling of plastic shopping bags. "Where's your mother?" I say to the window. I wonder where my husband is and worry that he'll return to the running car and I'll be gone. Another mystery played out in the shopping center parking lot. Then it hits me. As sure as I am that I'm not pregnant, I know that I locked the keys in our car. I turn to look at it idling, a soft spool of exhaust drifting over the trunk and into the darkening night.

My husband isn't at the car, and he's not jogging down the aisle, either. He always runs when it's cold outside, though I point out to him that this only makes it colder.

He always chooses a shorter, yet more intense, experience over a longer, mellower encounter with the troubles of this life. I wonder, too, if this is how he sees our marriage, an element to endure by sprinting through the milestones until there isn't anything left?

I don't flag down any other shoppers. I'm not sure what I could say to them, and I'd rather not get anyone else involved. So, I wait in the cold, my toes going numb, knowing that one of two things will happen: Either my husband will return carrying a single plastic bag with the smiley face winking on the front, or the baby's mother will creep cautiously up to the car. Both promise a confrontation, and I don't know if I can handle either one. It's bad enough leaving a dog alone in a car in this weather, but a baby is just too much. It's the kind of story you see on the news. The thought of cameras, being interviewed on live TV, makes me hope that my husband will return first. He'll be angry I left the car. He's always worried about my safety, as though the minute I leave the apartment someone will attack me. Tonight, he'll cite the temperature, tell me he is worried I'll catch a cold or pneumonia. He's big on pneumonia for some reason. The entire time, he'll be looking at my stomach but won't mention the word *baby*. I guess we've both grown superstitious over the last year. *Will we, won't we* is not a popular game in our home. Maybe, I want to tell him, it's not happening because our bodies don't think we're ready. He'd call that psychological bullshit. I'd call it an excuse I've made up to make myself feel better. I'm not sure why he won't let me lie to myself. That, I want to tell him, makes me human.

I decide then that until someone separates us, I'll only look down upon the baby and wait.

I kick at the ground, willing warmth into my foot. It catches the crushed-open lip of a Burger King cup. Soda and ice splatter against the stiff fabric of my jeans. The liquid freezes in a sticky spray around my knee. Annoyed, I kick my other foot into a pile of ice. The pieces carom off the tire and skitter across the cement where they come to rest near some candy-bar wrappers stuck to the ground by a brown oily substance. What is it about parking lots that people think they can leave their trash everywhere? I'm disgusted enough to walk away, but cold enough to know it will take hours before the feeling comes back into my toes. I stay.

The baby rocks, throws his hand in the air, and smiles. The drool collects in the corner of his mouth before cascading onto the zipper of his coat. "I can't do it," I say out loud. The whole thing is a mess.

His smile goes away, and his face turns solemn. The sound of feet pounding on the pavement, a gust of wind pulls at the hair tucked into my jacket, the hood flopping back, exposing my face to the elements.

"What are you doing?" a voice says. "Get away from there. Get!"

I turn toward the voice. The end of the cart bumps into my hip, knocking me back a step. I push the hair from my eyes. The woman in front of me is disheveled, her hair black and natty from being dyed too many times. She wears no coat but is dressed in one of those sweatsuits that are all one solid color. It's much too big for her, and the cloth billows in the wind like a tarp taped over a busted car window. Though she's young, there are lines on her face grooved into the skin like shattered glass. In her cart is a large box containing a space heater and a few shopping bags. A package of diapers pokes out from one of the bags.

"You can't leave a baby out here." I point to the window, then draw my arms to my chest, hugging myself, as if there isn't anything else to say.

"He was sleeping when I left. He is always sleeping." She leaned over the cart, resting her elbows on the handlebar, resigned to let me criticize her.

"I should report this," I say.

A security truck drives up the aisle, its orange light rotating over the hoods of the parked cars. The woman waits for it to pass, before saying, "Fine, report me. Here's your chance."

The truck gets to the front of the lane, stops for a couple pushing a cart laden with bag after bag of groceries. The truck turns left and idles down another aisle.

"You're like everyone else," the woman says. "You don't want to get involved, either. I do the best I can. You want to help? Let me get in the car and take him home. It'll be warm there now," she says, pushing the cart toward me.

I glance down at the baby, and I have to agree that he seems fine, that maybe I'm no better equipped to protect him than this woman. I put my hand on the glass, my fingertips the only trace that I've been standing there watching over him.

"Go on, now," she says. "He's not alone anymore."

"We're all alone," I say. I walk around the trunk of the car, head down, pulling tight the strings of my hood, careful to step around what's left of a runover banana.

Filaments of Air

I've got the sharp, little scissors palmed in my hand, and I'm waiting in line. Your brothers and sisters, your mother, they all went first. Chelsea, crying, her makeup streaking down her cheek like ink from a broken fountain pen. Your mother tucks Chase's beanie little head against her hip, and she's gasping for air. And maybe you finally did it, took away all the oxygen? Remember how we'd put those balloons to our lips, shrugging away the taste of latex, staring at our chests in the mirrors, our bird bodies taking the shape of women, until you gagged, the ball of air sputtering out of our fingers, racing around the room, before falling, limp, at our feet.

I made the mistake of hugging your mother before I asked for the snip of your hair. I could feel you whispering, "Ask first," but it was too late. The intimacy I had to trade was given freely, your mother leaching my little thread of power, mine and yours, bodies, so similar, down to the misshapen pinky toes, the nails like flattened pennies, our hair the same honeydew coloring that usually comes from a box. I was proud of her, your mom, for not saying your name, though I would have taken your place.

I'm alone up here, and it's the first time I've been close enough to see that your makeup is all wrong. That instead of scissors, I should have brought more foundation, an eyelash curler, certainly, some blush, a touch of lipstick, because I want to remember you smiling, crying from laughter, our stupid jokes making the walls of your house ring with our promised youth. But I've always been the selfish one, right? So I'm going to make use of these scissors, because why should the earth get the best of you? I skim the blades over the plush crèche of the casket lining, the points ripping the fabric subtly. The darkness will know I was here first.

I tug sharply, but you don't cry out. We've seen too many horror movies, joked too often about zombies, wondering why you couldn't look half-dead and gorgeous. If anyone had a chance, it was you. I take a plait of hair, wishing they had let me braid it. Your bangs sit awkwardly against your forehead. You look like one of those late-in-life movie starlets, reaching back for the summer of their ingénue fame—or a soccer mom on a Sunday morning, sipping her chamomile tea. The scissors jump in my hand, raking across that unnaturally flat space of skin, metal grinding, as the hair shreds into fine whispers of eyelashes, as I grab the larger pieces that dot your cheeks. I bend toward you, blowing, giving you my last filaments of air.

The Age of Quitters

Once a month, I bring a bucket of KFC to my father's house. Its greasy smells burrow further and further into the car fabric. On hot days, it's worse than cigarette smoke, a cloud of invisible depression layered over the car, turning any mood sour. I'm there today to take him to the doctor. An appointment I've rescheduled five times over the past year.

My father's house glowered atop a moldering hill that shaded the Tippecanoe River below. This was not the house I grew up in, but the one my dad found after my mother passed away. The floorboards rotted from the creeping humidity and yearly flooding from the brown water that whirled and pooled just out of sight from the kitchen window. Dad found the house the way a homeless man finds a coat, left behind due to rips and stains from the previous owner's disregard or laziness.

Dad, like usual, answered the knock with a yell, refusing to meet me at the front door. I weaved down the short hallway, stepped around piles of yellowing newspapers, and made my way into the dark living room, where I found him in his usual spot in the sunken recliner. Another one of his finds, the headrest poking from an industrial dumpster behind a PetSmart. Each month, he'd have some new piece of junk, his life outside of my visits a mystery.

"Chicken again?" He smiled, tongue poking out of the hole his missing tooth left behind. When I asked him about the tooth a year ago, he told me, "A goddamn quitter. Like your mom."

I had dropped the bucket of chicken then, wings and legs spilling out like broken marionettes, the smell of roasted meat making me gag. I'd walked out without saying another word. I sat in the car for an hour shining the headlights directly into the picture window of the dining room. I thought I saw the curtains move once, but it could have been from the air of the vent. It took me three months before I could buy another bucket of chicken and return. We don't talk much about my mother anymore. He cares too much about the chicken.

This time, I sat the bucket on the end table between us. I settled into the faded accent chair, the bright colors of its African safari blending together like a smeared painting.

"We've got that appointment in an hour. I don't think they will let me reschedule it again."

My father didn't answer, but skipped the plate and dug his hand into the bucket. In the interest of time, I went without the plate, too, picking up a leg. The chicken was wet and satisfying as we tore off hunks of meat and chewed mostly in silence.

"You see that fellow, there?" He pointed a machine-blunted finger at the TV screen, where a politician stood in front of a podium, his face red, arms waving vigorously at the crowd below.

"He any different than anybody else that wants to tell me what to do?" I asked.

"Probably not, but he might be. He talks an awful lot about family. How he grew up with hardnosed parents who taught him the value of work, the value of sitting down at the dinner table. Might be on to something."

"Definitely our type of guy," I said, enjoying the irony, my fingers glistening with grease. Blobs of chicken skin dotted my father's shirt, and I knew there was no way I'd get him to change it and still make the appointment on time. "Isn't he the one that wants to kick everyone different out of the country? Says it's the only way to get our jobs back?"

I rattled the box, two breast pieces, stuck to the bottom. I left them there for my father. My hope was that he'd save them for tomorrow, but I knew he threw them down the hill, bucket and all, trying, but failing. None of them ever making it to the river. I saw some of the boxes once when his air-conditioning unit was acting up, the boxes little burial sites of rotting food surrounded by tufts of grass a foot high. I didn't stop to inspect them, knowing that if I had, I'd have to ask questions. From the day he moved into this sad sack of a house, something changed in our relationship where we no longer talked about ourselves. He never asked about my job, a claims adjuster for an insurance company. He never asked about my wife, either. I think he was ashamed that we'd never had children. Afraid maybe that we were able, but had wantonly chosen against it. He was wrong and right, and I'd thought to correct him, but I liked our surface-level conversations about angry politicians and the price of corn, the way he tracked the local high school's football team, and deals on watermelons at the two supermarkets up the road. Getting him to go to the doctor went against that code.

We didn't talk about the status of his home, the leak in the roof above his bed that threatened to fill the entire ceiling with mold, or the layer of dust that coated even the kitchen counter, how the fast food was taking a toll on his body, his broad shoulders softening with age and saturated fat, his belly extending over his belt like a hill that was continually accumulating snow. I offered to help him clean the house once, and he turned up the TV loud enough to broadcast a baseball game to the whole neighborhood. I left that night with a headache. My father's lasting skill was to eliminate conversations he didn't want to have. Immature, sure, but effective.

But I couldn't stand by and watch him self-destruct. "Actually, Dad, could you turn the channel. I've got something to say." I wiped my hands on the arms of the chair. A habit I had picked up from spending so much time in this ramshackle house.

"He's got something to say," my father said to the room. But he changed the channel, flicking through color-drenched scenes of reality and fantasy until he landed on the Little League World Series. Sports had always opened a safe, muted space between us, as neither of us had played them much, and there were no regrets about winning or losing between us. "Get on with it, Evan. People got lives to think about."

"I'm moving, Dad," I said, letting the words hang there. A trick I was sure he would see right through, but in the silence I started to think that maybe I should move.

On the screen a ten-year-old swings and strikes out, the opposing team running toward the mound, mobbing the pitcher.

"Poor bastard," my father said, real sorrow clutching at his words. "You finally saved enough for the big house, huh? You thinking Cherry Hill or The Reserve? Personally, I'd prefer building off in the woods down near 350 West, but I know how that wife of yours likes being surrounded by people. I'm not criticizing. Hell, your mother loved the neighbors, too. It gave her something to do. I was damn well thankful for that, you understand." He takes a breath and something rattles in his chest like the BB in the bottom of a spray-paint can.

When he mentions my mother now, fear and anxiety

well up, a feeling like walking in the dark. "We're going to Pennsylvania. Just outside of Philly. Maybe a twenty-minute drive to downtown."

"Your mother loved it *here*. You understand that, right?"

"I do, Dad." We both shift our focus to the screen. A rare double play, the defense excited, clutching at each other, as they run off the field, ready to hit with new confidence. I wonder if I've ever felt that happy before. "You ever been that happy?" I ask, pointing toward the TV.

"If I have, I don't remember. Wouldn't know where to look for it now." My father picks at the space between his front teeth with the blade of his pocket knife. A habit that I swear he's picked up just to shock me.

I flinch but don't say anything about it. Another dead end. One of the hundreds of small reasons I'm moving. "Say you could find it. Say you thought it might be out there somewhere."

"You think it's in Philly? There's a reason it's not the capital anymore."

"It's not really important where. Philly just happens to be one of the hubs for the company I work for," I say, standing, but not quite ready to walk away. "Look, I've got to move on."

"From the living or the dead? Because I'm all that's left. You remember that?" He tries to stand, too, but he can't rock himself out of the chair.

"This is what I'm talking about."

"Talking? You haven't said a word. You come in here and say you're moving. I'm supposed to, what, shake your hand, give you a pat on the back?"

How many conversations have I had with myself, pretending I know what he'll say, working the words over in my head, telling him exactly what I think he needs to do to get his life back in order. And none of it, I realize, counts for anything. "You're right. I can't talk to you. I don't know how."

A dozen memories, none of them distinct except the image of me running to my mother with some grievance about my father. He yelled at me to shut up, he lost his patience when he was teaching me to drive, the time he lost his wallet and blamed it on me—every one of those times I went to my mother. I begged her to talk to him, asked her to leave me out of it, asked her to protect me from his anger or his indifference to change, to the acknowledgment of my feelings.

"You could have done that." He points to the screen. The ball bounces cleanly into the third baseman's glove. The player fires a rocket to first. Another inning over.

"I was horrible. I couldn't catch the ball. The whole thing terrified me. But really that's besides the point."

"Could have been good at other things, too. Your mother let you quit everything."

I paced in front of the TV, arms crossed. "She was trying to help me. Don't you get that? Her whole life she tried to take care of us. And now look at you."

I stood over him, feet unbalanced on the stacks of magazines next to his chair, the wadded tissues, crusty with snot. On his shirt, a single piece of miss-chewed chicken skin rested against the fabric. I fought the urge to pluck it away.

My father spoke in a low voice, words clip-clopping out of his mouth, "This is the life I've chosen. I know you don't like it, but I won't be bullied by you or your mother."

"Bullied? You sound like a teenager. Live like one, too." I picked up a sweat-crusted pair of socks and dangled them in front of his face. How is it that our family so easily brings out the worst in us?

"You want to leave? I've survived worse. I'll live longer than you could ever imagine. I'm no quitter," he said, closed-fist pounding his chest twice. He pointed the remote at me and then waved me to the side, flipping the channel back to the angry politician.

I've been dismissed, and yet I stayed, sitting down in my chair. The man at the podium smiled sarcastically, while he threw out one liners about healthcare and war. He was so sure of himself, while I lived in the limbo of finally telling my father a fraction of how I felt, and wondering if it had made any difference.

"Will you at least get in the car? I'd feel better …"

"You run away. I suppose that's your right. But leave all the rest of it alone. Hate me, if you want, but I think I deserve that much—to be left alone."

"You're willing to die here. Like this."

"Son, it's as good a place as any."

I sit there for a few minutes thinking that maybe he's right. That even this move to Philly is some kind of death, that all change is a step toward not immortality, but the quickening of the end. But it's my choice, so even though I reach in for another piece of chicken, the grease, just another layer of life that can be washed away, I'm already calculating how quickly I can move on. "You're killing yourself," I said.

He grinned, Cheshire creepy, telling me, "No faster than anyone else."

Airbrushed

(The Bridge, Part 3)

At the start of eighth grade, you say we gotta cool it. I accuse you of watching too many gangster films again, but you shrug your shoulders. "Those are the breaks, kid," you say, giving me a wink that I know you've spent hours practicing in front of the mirror.

You say this to me while we're sitting on the porch swing, our feet dangling from the bench, the chain squeaking as we glide forward and back, your hand intertwined with mine because we were again practicing the girlfriend-boyfriend project, so we'd be ready when we found our true loves. Everything was cool until I brought our tangled hands up to scratch my nose. I didn't know this in the moment, but truthfully, I wanted to do everything together, coupled like the number eleven.

"You ever just want to run away," you said, pulling at your shirt collar with both hands. Your collarbone poked out like the Y of a nice climbing tree. I imagined ants marching along that ridge because I knew you'd never let me get that close. You were having another one of your suffocating moments. These were happening more frequently, and I had run out of ways to keep you from leaving.

You lurched out of the swing, chains popping, saying you had to go, that I shouldn't call, that maybe you'd find your sister after all.

"Candy," I said, standing until the swing caught the back of my knees.

"If you can't say it now, Gavin, I don't think you ever will."

I thought of everything but *I love you* because that's what fathers and mothers said to each other as they left the house every morning to go to work. I needed you more than a flimsy kiss on the forehead, more than the I'll-take-care-of-you-by-paying-the-bills kind of Monday-morning slow dance.

"I love the way your knees poke out of the holes in your jeans," I said. "I love the way your hair whips around in the wind and always lands in the corner of your mouth. I love the way your ankles crack when you walk down the steps."

When you reach the dividing line of our properties, the spray-painted fluorescent-orange slashes from the city works department create a line I can't cross. "You only love the pictures-in-a-magazine parts of me, Gavin. I don't want to be airbrushed my whole life."

You've folded your arms over your chest, and your elbows, exposed, sore and scabbed from your last skateboarding attempts. I'd like to put my tongue in the hollow of your pain. But I can only reach for your face, aiming for the lazy strands of hair curving around your cheek. I'm tightrope-walking around the circumference of the moon while you walk away, middle finger raised, torching the earth between us.

Righteous,
Dapper, Famous

Us boys stood in a semicircle on the wooden stage they had built for the ceremony, squinting into the sun. The man with the camera checked his film. The paint was still sticky around our feet, the American-flag bunting freshly strewn across the front. We were a restless bunch, not much good at waiting. None of us were used to standing in front of a crowd so large, either. People coming in for the Easter-egg hunt after the ceremony. Little girls in taffeta dresses and little boys dressed in miniature suits, straining against their parents' grips, wanting to join us on stage. Us boys had never been so famous, standing there wondering how much we'd be rewarded.

Each of us was there, standing in the shadow of the limestone courthouse, to receive a certificate and a handshake, hoping for some money for helping to stop or report a crime. Timmy Thompson with his crooked eyes and big-as-horse teeth informed on his cousins and their brash uprooting of several stop signs three miles out of town. Bart

Hamilton, his red hair cut down to the length of comb bristles, saved a couple of cats from a rotted-out tree, though no one's sure he didn't put them there himself. The rest of us did similar good deeds, mowing and sweeping dust for nickels and dimes we donated to the church or the Salvation Army. Except for me, it's all pretty normal, off-the-cob, Bible-school kind of good deeds.

In the middle of our group, perched atop a hidden milk crate, stood a short, knife-blade-thin man named Purvis, with a togged-to-the-bricks freshly pressed suit, his smile as fake as the bank's insurance. We don't know what this phrase means, exactly, but when our daddies get drunk, they like to holler it at one another.

"Must want to be politicians," our daddies said as they hitched up their pants. The metal from the buckle and the leather strap of their belts have all been sold for half a week's worth of produce. Before we left for the center of town, they swirled the smoke from their cigarettes in our faces, hoping it would shield us from catching the smarmy-doughboy, do-gooder bug that was sure to follow us once we had shaken that politician's hand.

"F, B, I," we said slowly, our breath catching on each letter. We thought we knew the difference between us and the law, that we'd be a part of something new, that standing on that stage would elevate us above the scrapping and scraping for the meager leftovers from callous men.

A live microphone was set up to our left, and we were all dying to shout into it, convinced our voices would travel through time and space to radios all over the country. The camera was flashing and us boys smiled, hands pumping as the FBI man gripped our sticky fingers. I was standing last in line, next to a couple of tough-looking men, also in suits and clean-shaven. The smell of danger swirled around them, a tinge of gun oil, and it reminded me of my own daddy's shotgun. With tight lips, they gave the FBI man advice: "Smile, Little Mel. Old Hoover is watching. Take a knee, why don't you? You're in the spotlight now, Purvis. The face of the entire department."

Purvis ignored them, though his face started to look like a tomato. And when I stood next to him, the sun blocked for a second by his wide-brimmed hat, I could see the strain on his face. I didn't know those men, but I was proud to stand there with someone so calm, so focused. This was what us boys hoped to be when we got older. Righteous. Dapper. Famous. He leaned in close, his after-shave smelling like coconuts, the rest of him like sweat from one of my wrung-out shirts after chores, and there was a glimmer of the charade, before he asked me, "Son, remind me what you did?"

I don't lie much, but I'd been around adults enough to know a good opportunity when I saw one. "I stopped a coy-ote from stealing some chickens," I said.

The camera flashed. The man they called Purvis started to stand, but I tugged on his hand.

"Boy, is that all you've got? All these people out here to hear some farm boy and his nighttime hallucinations?"

"You want a better story? Is that what you's saying?"

The cameraman stepped in front of his camera, wiping his brow with a handkerchief. "That's all I need from you boys."

"Last chance, son," Purvis said. "The world is watch-ing."

On tiptoe, my head bobbed below the microphone. All those people looking at me, shading their eyes from the sun, expecting something. "I stopped that John Dillinger from robbing Bloom's IGA. Held him up with my sling-shot, I did. Told him, next time I'd put a rock right between his eyes."

A swell of sound comes from the crowd, my daddy standing in the middle, shaking his head. I'm smiling because I've got the whole world listening. Surely, they're broadcasting my voice across the country.

Before I could say another word, that small man was yanking me away, turning me toward the sight of the rest of them boys jumping off the stage. Scattering like corn seed, not a one of them looking back as they dispersed into the crowd. The larger men stepped forward, suits creaking like sun-cracked leather, arms reaching out, murder written all over their faces. I ducked behind Purvis and knocked over the microphone, static crackling from the speakers like gunfire over the radio. The crowd recoiled, kicking up dust, backing away from the beating I surely had coming.

Purvis held up his hands, and the suits stopped just out of reach from my bobbing head. In the confusion, a pair of hands gripped my arms and hauled me off the stage. My fear mellowed as I caught a whiff of my father's smoked skin, the familiar scratch of his sideburns against my cheek. The camera flashed behind us, the light winking out like a snuffed candle.

Daddy planted me on the ground, before lurching onto the stage. He started swinging his fists while he was still on his knees. Purvis hollering, "Now, wait just a minute. Wait."

But it was too late. Those large men were piling on Daddy like he had stolen a loaf of bread from the IGA. Daddy didn't give in so easily, and the whole mess of men rolled around that stage cussing and carrying on. People in the crowd, men mostly, cheering like it was a cockfight. Until finally they rolled off the edge, feet and arms catching in that bunting, ripping it as they fell in a heap on the dusty ground. They looked like a pregnant heifer laying on its side, breathing heavily, its stomach knotted in pain.

Purvis stood above them, his arms crossed. "I hope you're happy, son."

And strangely I was. I didn't have any idea of what I

had set in motion, but my daddy was willing to throw a punch for me, and I couldn't wait to hear my own voice coming through the radio later that night.

The two men scooted away from my father, the lapels of their suits ripped and sagging, their breath whistling through their teeth, some blood dripping from their noses.

"Arrest him already, Melvin."

Daddy got to his feet, head stuck between his knees. But his clothes, already dusty and ragged before the fight, didn't look any worse than when he'd put them on this morning.

"Yeah, Purvis. The crazy son of a bitch about broke my tooth."

"And make things worse?" Purvis said. "Hoover will send me back to the coast for this screwup. Up, now. Both of you. Shake this man's hand, before these people get any ideas."

Instead of heading home, my father led us toward the center of town, ducking through the crowd, his right eye swelling. My feet skipped over the dirt-patched road as I kept up with the lurching rhythm of his strides. We stopped on the sidewalk outside of Tiffany's Diner, and he put his arm around my shoulders.

"Goddamn, I didn't think you had it in you. Standing up to the law like that."

"I was just trying to get on the radio," I said, staring at my streaked reflection in the restaurant glass. Next to my face, on yellowed paper, one end curling inward, was the Wanted poster. *$5,000 Reward*. I hadn't known much about money back then because it was rarely in my possession, but I knew what those zeros would mean for our farm.

"Doesn't matter the reason. You gave 'em hell, son. Something people won't soon forget."

"I hope he does come. That Dillinger. I'm ready for him."

My father held open the door to the diner, and a whiff of cooler air waved against my face. The lights were off, but people were talking softly, raising sandwiches and coffee mugs to their faces.

He directed me toward a booth in the back, people turning their heads as I passed, whispering my name, a few older gentlemen stopping me to shake my hand, their eyes holding mine, before glancing back to their coffee mugs. My little lie had done more than stir up a little dust—a thing like that moved through town faster than a traveling Bible salesman.

While I waited, I watched my daddy talk to the cook at the counter. Daddy was negotiating something, his body in motion, hands cutting through the air like fan blades. He did everything but spit on the floor.

After a few minutes, he came back with two plates, piled high with french fries and burgers that were still sizzling from the grill. I couldn't remember the last time we'd ate anywhere outside of our house. My mother was always bent over a pot of boiling potato skins.

"Here's your reward, son." Daddy handed me the plate, the dirt from my hands soiling the white porcelain. "And by God, I hope you meet him someday. You could learn a thing or two from a man like that." My father, with his bruised lip and a small cut above his eye, chewed his burger and smiled. "Dig in. Dig in," he said, but I couldn't look away.

His face was a spectacle of satisfaction as the ketchup and mustard ran down his chin in glistening tears. I waited until he pushed his plate away from his chest and wiped his mouth. I took a bite, and though it was no longer hot, it was just as good as I imagined. My father watched me eat as if I were a gathering storm with enough rain to last the summer.

When Mono Was Part of the Equation

I'm in the back of the band room, sipping vodka from a dented Sprite bottle, avoiding Christopher Mackley and his overly earnest attempts to get me to buy something for the FFA fundraiser. Instruments, scratched and dull, smelling of melting crayons, threaten to tumble from their unsecured spots and give away my position in the closet. I've been coming here, ten minutes after the final bell, pulling open the door, my "teacher voice" caught on the upswing of my breath, a rhythm the band instructor would spend time correcting if I were one of his students. I always expect to catch a couple kissing or groping, but these kids lack imagination. It's all blurry pics of their stomachs shared on Snapchat or *Fortnite* dances and memes. The digital desperation of fake feelings taking over their lives. Middle schoolers have always been staging the fear and bravado of the early teen years, but now their actions seldom risk personal contact. High fives and furtive hugs replaced by the touch of chattering keyboards and smeared screens.

The cases of mono have been replaced by technological viruses, and so I'm often left alone with this closet of instruments.

I don't know what it says about me, this getting drunk in the closet of the band room, my own phone resting in the palm of my hand as I scroll through pictures of my ex-wife and her new boyfriend taking my kids to parades and pumpkin patches. My wife is in all of the pictures now, her rounded cheeks full of color and what I guess is happiness. Stock photos for two-dollar-picture-frame kind of joy. The kids are there, too, holding hands, looking admiringly back at the photographer, this man whose hands smell of corn and soil, who wishes me well with his words while his eyes always appraise my face as if I were just another animal he'd have to vaccinate.

Last week, after getting the kids in the car, and shaking his hand. My wife—ex, that is—was sick, apparently.

"A cough with a lot of phlegm," he tells me. "Fever, and just too tired. You understand," he says.

"Mono?" I ask hopefully.

"The kissing disease?" he asks, shaking my hand for the fifth time.

"The kids at school," I start, but I never know what to say.

The kids are fogging up the windows, pulling at each other's hair, their voices chittering like monkeys, shouting the name of the restaurant with the play place and the dollar menu. And I'm thinking: Maybe the joke's on me, because I showed up sober, promised myself I'd make it all weekend. Playing Barbies, watching *Moana* for the forty-seventh time, braiding their hair, and biting my tongue every time they said this man's name, voices reverent like talking about the Jesus of their Sunday-school stories.

"Listen, Cal," I say. "I know this is unusual, but maybe you've got a couple of bills in that wallet?"

"Say no more, James." He pulls out two twenties, puts them in the pocket of my dress shirt, gives my chest a pat. "Anything for the kids, am I right?" he says a little too loudly.

I glance over my shoulder and the girls are prairie-dogged over the back seat of the car, noses pushing against the window, and even if Cal won't say anything to my wife, the kids will. Someone's always watching, waiting for me to slip up, hoping to drag me under. And even if I deserve it, when will it ever end? You try to hold up under the scrutiny of six hundred middle schoolers, none of whom really want to learn, all of them with phones at the ready to film your latest fuckup.

Cal's looking at me closely, probably going through some checklist, marking me off for all the ways I'm a lesser man. Divorce opens a man up to a subset of strangers, men I'd never approach in public, much less shake hands with. I duck my head, feigning shame, mentally dividing the cash into separate opportunities as I get into the car. The girls are back to wrestling and chittering in the back seat. A little dinner for the kids, a cheap bottle to get me through the week, and the cheapest basket of oranges from the fundraiser. No more hiding in the band room closet, hiding from the Christopher Mackleys of the world.

"*No more*," I say, and the girls get quiet, and finally I've got their attention. I don't know what to say next, but I'm a teacher, so if I give it a minute, something's bound to come to mind.

Open to an Ocean

He circles the fountain like an animal pushed out of its habitat. The heat smothers his body. It's the tenth day above ninety, and still they—the powerful men he imagines sitting in a tall building, chewing on ice and swiveling in office chairs with leather seats that cool the men's backs as they laugh at little boys like him—won't open the water-tower reserves. He flaps his hands at the sun, but it trains its unforgiving eye on his narrow shoulders. He's heard about invisible rays, but today they punch and slap, making his skin as tight as the tops of conga drums.

His mother calls to him from their lofty apartment until her voice breaks. It's even hotter in the room he shares with his uncle and older brother. They pass a cigarette back and forth, argue about politics that they are too poor to change, their words pouting in the rising smoke.

"Go play," they say. "Be a kid, Damian."

He wants to ask them why he can't be a kid in his room, one who colors or reads books, who gets to lie in the bed for once and not on the pile of blankets on the floor. Why must he have to run and jump, and be the plaything of gnats and wasps?

But they bully him with their bodies, their sloping shoulders and cantaloupe necks, their voices chasing him out the door and into the street. Though he mingles with trash and dust in the street, there is space to twirl, to hoot, and to cry behind the grocer's dumpsters because he can't reach the lids.

The alleys offer shadows, the closest he can come to sunblock, but there are noises of machines and of ghouls, legends of harm that take him back to the fountain. He scuffs his feet along the path, wishing the bricks were wedges of cheese or sliced watermelon. He bends his head over his knees and sniffs. He waits for the birds, but they no longer linger or scuttle across the path, no longer squawk for a piece of bread. They hide somewhere not so far away, but still, they remain unreachable. Like the river of his mother's eyes where the happiness has receded from the banks, making everything dull with dried dirt.

And still, she calls for him, because even without water, even with the searing heat, her instinct is to love him, and so he dances. Soft humming from the well of his lungs gives him rhythm, round and round the spigot buried beneath the brick. Faster his body lurches, arms raised toward the sky in a toddler's desperation, until the people gather around him, air springing from their lips. The ground shakes beneath his feet, soles of his shoes clopping, echoing, calling for his mother to join him.

Two, three days, he keeps watch for his mother, the people babbling her name, though he's never spoken it out loud. They are connected like a string between tin cans, vibrations from his dance catching on the wind. A sound so shrill that his mother almost falls from her window as she leans toward him, ready to receive the pieces of him he's willing to sacrifice for these first drops of rain, her tears running rustily down her cheek.

The people shout, "Now, boy, you've done it," and "Don't stop!" and "They won't ignore us now."

But they do, these men in their towers, lazing in their

pools, watching with frozen grins until the boy collapses. Only then do they relent, a swipe of a hand, and their machines come alive, sending a streaking signal toward the ground, quick as lightning but soundless, as the pipes gurgle and then gush, the fountain erupting. The mother wades through the crowd, women parting, children hiccuping as they are held back until this mother touches her child near his neck, water seething around his nose and mouth. His eyes open to an ocean.

Stitches Unraveling

We're in his old hometown, where the buildings sag on their foundations, and the metal siding of the 70s is rusting, sun-scorched, and dusty from cornfield weed killer. "Lucky we didn't all get cancer," he says, pulling out the tassel from a female corn plant. He shows me this trick every time we get near a stalk of corn. I'm forty years old, and he's still trying to impress me with these preteen magic tricks.

He's going in for some tests tomorrow. The kind where they poke and prod, scoop out blood from your veins like grape jelly, then make you wait two weeks for the results. Bone disease, MS, arthritis, everything is possible when they open you up and shine a light into the cave of arteries and sinews, God's stitching unraveling.

We stand in front of the press box that leans over the T-ball field like a disapproving teacher, ready to correct an unlucky student's grammar mistakes.

"I got my first hit right there," he says.

I have to stop myself from reciting the lines of a movie I've already seen fifty times.

"A looper over the second basemen's head. I watched it roll through the clover. Startled into running the bases when everyone started yelling. Frantic," he says, picking up a piece of gravel the color of a rotisserie chicken. The clouds puffy and white like a steaming pile of mashed potatoes.

I'm hungry, but I can't say anything yet. He's thrown himself into the pool of nostalgia, and I can't help him swim through it.

He kicks the metal fencing of the backstop, his hands gripping the chain-link. "My dad volunteered to announce the games. No color commentary back then. Just who's up to bat, who's on deck."

"One time," I say, arms crossed, but he's already taking his place at home plate, pretending to swing a bat, elbow up just like his father taught him. "Sexy," I say, but he just nods. "Carlson's up to bat, swinging for the fences," I yell, my voice cracking.

I wait for someone to tell us to leave, but no one comes, and I'm stuck here for as long as his memory holds, for as long as he can still raise that elbow, run these bases. My voice continually cracking, following the arc of an invisible ball rolling through the clover.

Knocking

on doors in the middle of the night had become essential. We weren't sleeping, anyway. Blood spiked with sugar from shotgunning cans of Mountain Dew, *Beavis and Butt-Head* was too stupid even to laugh at. Truth or Dare meant nothing when we already told each other everything, so the dare at every Saturday sleepover was the knocking.

After midnight, we cut the music, dropped the lights, and lay head to head, shoulders covered by neon-colored nightgowns, while our legs sweated beneath the twin fabrics of our leggings and the shimmery padding of our sleeping bags. We practiced calming our breathing, hearts hammering, waiting for Gwen's or Justina's mom to do the final check before they drifted down the hall to their own beds. The dads plodded down the hall, never stopping at the bedroom door, never saying goodnight.

A year ago, Kelsey's dad sat on the corner of her bed at one in the morning and sang us love songs, his voice weepy, his busted knuckles creaking as he gripped the comforter. We didn't go out that night. We kicked and elbowed each other, keeping everyone awake, not knowing what would happen if we all fell asleep. Eventually his voice hitched, and he whispered, *Goodnight now, goodnight.* Kelsey apologized, said he just missed her mom, said it wasn't fair that he was so sad, and could they just go to sleep? Everyone nodded and faked sleep, until dawn, each of us calling our own mothers, asking to come home.

Kelsey was no longer invited. We didn't have time for sadness, for unpredictable fathers, for Saturday nights spent sleeping. We had to knock and shriek and run and hide behind mailboxes and China grasses that had grown willowy at the edge of winter-split driveways first paved in the 60s. Only here were we brave enough to face these men, our fathers and neighbors, their legs naked but dusted with hair, stomachs rounded from stress and beer, hair sprouted in different directions, their arms lifted in fists, striking out at invisible phantoms. Bewildered and angry, from a distance, they had never looked so safe.

Covenants

No one knew how the back windshield got cracked, but she loved the way the dying sunlight filtered through the spiderwebbed fractures. If she tilted her head just right, she could see the full prism of Earth, feel the shaky tug of gravity as they spun through time and space, the truck rocketing over dirt roads, leaving behind the fields of fragile cornstalks.

This was their third new town this month. They raced ahead of the swirling dust that chased them through tornado alley. When they made it to the Mississippi, that great snake of water, she thought they'd found the edge of the world and that surely their migration was over.

But with dirt-stained hands in her lap, she pulled at a new rip in her last skirt. Her father drifted across the one-lane road, her mother's rhythmic gasps jarring him awake in time to jerk the wheel. They drove through the night toward a new destination without the promise of work or food.

When they parked in the Methodist church parking lot somewhere south of Chicago, she thought maybe tonight they would find a bed with fresh sheets to sleep in. Instead, her mother shushed her, taking out the family Bible, reading about the multitude of God's covenants with his people in the accumulating twilight.

"There are no more promises," her mother said.

"Mother, what did we do this time?" she asked.

Her mother took her hands, skimming the rough lye soap over her fingernails. "We dared, child. We dared."

If It Weren't for the Lights

Hurricane Jacob prowls across the meteorologist's map, but I've been disappointed by every man I've known, so I refuse to evacuate. I've opened all the windows to watch the rain pop and sizzle on the laminate floors. It's not long before your bobbleheads find a current leading them out the front door and down the driveway. "Collectibles" you called them when we didn't have enough money to eat, when we had to shit in the McDonald's bathroom because we'd run out of toilet paper. I begged you to sell the comic books—yes, even the ones featuring Spider-Man—but you traded them for courtside seats to a losing basketball team, sharing nachos with a former pop star, the one we *had* to name our daughter after, the daughter you see only on holidays that don't involve gifts.

That's okay. The action figures made a great faux Nativity, with Darth Vader presiding over the sacred birth of Yoda to Han Solo and Princess Leia as parents, while Chewbacca served nicely as the only wise man. It was too annoying to find two more wise men, and one was already more than enough.

When the boat finally comes, its small motor sounding like the serene rumbling of our refrigerator on sleepless nights, our daughter and I are on the roof of the house you abandoned. We wave your limited-edition replica lightsabers. In the gloaming, our daughter's face brightens. She thinks you've come back, that all men have the potential to be her daddy. That men leave for important reasons, that men have just as many motives to return.

The bearded old captain guides his boat toward the dormer windows. "You all are lucky," he shouts, flinging a rope. "I saw your toys from miles away. Nothing else would have caught my attention."

I offer the lightsabers as a reward, but he waves me off. "Ought to stay close to the things that keep us alive," he says, piloting us farther into our neighborhood—which looks more like the ocean, the landmarks aquariumed by the flood.

The water teems with colorful debris. Legos bob like candy sprinkles on a giant sludge of baking cake. The boat speeds up, troweling through the confettied remains of your card collection; the bloated faces of sports stars paste against its sides, while swirling countercurrents claim the bodies of G.I. Joes and Power Rangers rather than our own.

"Close your eyes," I warn my daughter, hoping to ward off the riches of destruction.

If Even the Angels

The bricks of the blood-stained streets glistened like roasting hams, but all the glazier could smell was the rotten fruit of unpicked orchards and lonesome vineyards. He hobbled through the twisting concrete corridors with the six-paned window riding across his back, his last partition of glass. The leaded edge of the glass developed a slippery gloss in his hands, but he knew this was better than the smell of gun oil, the heft of the steel barrel. Months ago, when the sounds of war were still far off, his son had demonstrated how to hold a new rifle, how to pull back the bolt, how to line up the sights. His son, like most of the able-bodied men of this generation, was lost to the idolatry of war—injured, imprisoned, or missing in the lust of vengeance. And now the glazier vowed to find him.

While no one asked specifically for the glass, this was all the glazier had to trade for information, for hope. He called out, voice echoing like the somber sound of an untuned piano. The few people brave enough to stick out their heads shouted at him, gesturing to the crumbling foundations and fractured glass refracting the dawn sunlight. Bring us water, bring us bread, they demanded before moling back into their burrows.

The glazier walked on, the tips of his boots soaking,

until he came across a few knots of people. Women weeping openly, men's faces shadowed, their voices a dark tangle of despair. They offered nothing more than the rumors of injured soldiers that kept his legs scuffling forward.

A cut-glass memory of his son at eight, dancing in the rain, tongue lizarding out for a taste of the crying sky. The glazier's work never-ending. In those days, the boy stood in the haze of the fire, restless but attentive to the shapes of blown glass. Those fires gone, the glazier was left with the cold sweat of his journey.

In the town center, the church long abandoned, the storied stained glass, fractured kaleidoscopes scattered through the yellowing grass. Crudely painted letters of liberation bristled across blackened stone walls. He stopped, the muscles in the back of his knees arched, a bridge poorly constructed. He wanted a moment to rest, to consider, but if even the angels were against the church, the glazier would find somewhere else to rest.

The concussive sound of mortar fire echoed across the pavers, leading him out of the city and toward enemy lines. At the last façade, he gave in to the demands of the weighted glass. A crab abandoning its shell, he leaned the glass against the dusty concrete. The sun flared upon its leaded edge. The glazier resigned himself to this post—a human baluster waiting for the men to return. Surely, something —the scent of bread, the ghost of a voice, a flash of dappled light catching—would guide them home. His son's delicate fingers, fit for the piano or the scalpel, thrust firmly in the pocket of his jacket until the squint of recognition brought the boy's hands skyward, waving.

Candy:
A Teenage Gospel
(The Bridge, Part 4)

On those days that neither of us felt like living, we bought candy cigarettes and Twinkies, drank soda until our eyes swam rheumy, and dangled our feet over the wooden bridge, promising each other we'd be the first to jump, that the one left high above would watch the other until there was no more struggle against the current. "Look for the air bubbles," you said, hands pulling out your ponytail for the eighth time that morning. Fifteen, but so small, I knew you wouldn't make a splash, a dragonfly finally landing, coasting down the river, the fallen queen of a Coors Light box. I played along because I'd let you get away with anything, even death.

I promised I wouldn't follow, that I'd have to stay alive, because the people would demand a witness. Sure, they'd blame me, but you thought I was strong enough to take it. The accusations, the threats, the whispers, and the stares, the way adults would look at me sideways, wondering. "You'll be famous, Gavin. Famous is always better than dead."

I had promised I wouldn't love you, either, that I would not keep the strings of hair I cut away the time we got lost in the woods, the ratty strands caught on a grasping tree limb, the one we thought had come alive for those frightful seconds. You hugging yourself, elbows rubbed raw from cutting our own trail, you swearing the river road was just around the next hill. The little dot of blood on your cheek, a dollop of frosting I couldn't resist.

"If you're gonna kiss me, you better do it now. I can't escape or nothing."

"Let me just get my knife," I said, because even though your words said yes, I knew you really meant no.

"We agreed it had to be the river."

"I'm just cutting you loose, Candy," I said. Maybe even then I knew, goosebumps and that waving in and out sensation of first love.

The day it happened, the day you didn't float, the day you didn't wait for me, the sheriff showed up at my door. I'll admit, for once, I wasn't thinking about you. Your crooked smile with those bucky rabbit teeth, the way your knees turned in toward one another, how your breath always smelled like a Jolly Rancher baking in the sun. No, I was playing *Sonic*, battling my way into the Metropolis level, thumbs aching from pressing so hard on the controller, caught up in the blur of colors, collecting rings.

They sat me down in the living room, my mother wadding her robe in her hands, not even apologizing for the state of our house, the fact that she hadn't gotten dressed yet, the bowls of half-eaten cereal, the milk gray and warming.

After the sheriff cleared his throat for about the tenth time, I said, "I was supposed to be there."

"Where, son?"

"At the river. That's what this is about, right? Tell me Candy sent you. Tell me it's a joke." My voice cracked, and I remembered the way you used to mock me, your voice going higher and higher until I laughed, pushing your shoulder away because I couldn't handle being so close.

"Honey, there's been an accident," my mother said.

"Oh, you can do better than that, Mom," I said, bouncing up, headed toward the kitchen.

"Gavin," the man said, as if my name were the source of his exhaustion. "We need to talk about Candy."

"If you'd just go get her," I started, but my mom's hand was on the back of my neck, and the sheriff looked away. "I should hit you," I whispered.

The sheriff didn't move, didn't reach for his gun, would not even look at my face.

If it had been a joke, you would have begged him for more flair. He would have waved you away, citing regulations about unholstering his gun. His resolve, though, wouldn't have lasted more than a minute. Your tilted eyebrows would have said it all. *I know you've already fallen in love with me, so do this one thing for me.*

But love never guaranteed breathing or floating or safety or pride in being alive or the last-second remembrance of your voice, all gone like the final drop of water circling the rim of a drain.

•

You said I'd be famous, but everyone hated me instead. I was sitting in the same desk, the one in front of me vacated by your accident. The counselor, Mr. Jenkins, encouraged me to say suicide, but what the fuck does he know? "We had plans," I told him a week after the funeral. His bald head turned all red, and he couldn't get any words out. I almost laughed. You would have done something crazy like kissed his cheek or jumped on the sofa, but I wasn't allowed to laugh or cough or especially cry. Those were the new rules I gave myself.

So the adults all watched me pretty closely, taking away scissors, standing outside the bathroom door. They looked at me like I was a dehydrated plant. That words were like water, and I needed more chances to speak about my feelings. So much bullshit attention, right? The other students hated it. Nobody could do anything bad enough to fill the void. I was like a black hole sucking in all this adult energy.

Grant, that half-brained jock who wanted to take you to the dance. You remember? The one who kept flipping the hair out of his eyes, pursing his lips like he was smoking, but he didn't even have a vape? He tells me that some of the juniors have been talking about "getting" me. Drowning me in the river if you can believe it.

"They said they gotta make it right," Grant said. "Balance the universe. Avenge Candy."

"Like they knew her," I said, slamming my locker shut. Don't worry I took out that picture of you and me falling out of the bounce house.

"You could move," Grant said. "Run away, at least. My dad said trouble is going to find you."

"Wouldn't take a psychic," I said. I walked down the hall, staring at the muddy toes of my shoes. Most nights I snuck out to the river, stepping over rocks and beer bottles, wishing you believed in ghosts.

•

One night the juniors caught me on the edge of the bridge. I was coming back from the gun club, a bunch of shotgun shells in my pockets. I was planning on throwing them into the river, watching them float away. I was thinking maybe I could fill the whole thing up with junk, stop the current. It won't bring you back, but neither will doing my homework or mowing the yard, talking about my feelings or slitting my wrists. The counselor calls this acceptance, but I don't have words yet for wanting to destroy everything. I watch videos of buildings blowing up until I fall asleep. My parents hover near my bedroom, but they don't say anything. They won't even say your name. To everyone else, it's like you were never here.

But the juniors, right? I was hoping for something more like *West Side Story*—knives or chains, maybe a baseball bat. Only one of them was wearing a letterman's jacket. They held their phones out in front of them, flashlights like golden orbs dancing as the bridge shook from their weighted steps. It should have been like a duel from the Wild West, but it was more like seeing people from church in the grocery store. I would have stepped around them, but their faces were too earnest. They had shit they wanted to say, and I was the only audience.

"This thing is a piece of shit. Why would anyone hang out here?" the one in the letter jacket said. He was taller than the rest, but skinny, a giraffe among these other animals.

"You shouldn't be here," I said, taking a shell out of my pocket and tossing it over the rail. The glow of one of their flashlights tracked it to the water.

"Dude, what the hell was that?"

"I think he's got a gun."

I turn toward them because this was the stupidest thing I had ever heard. "If I had a gun, you think I'd be standing here?"

"Just tell us how it happened," the one in front said, the frames of his glasses catching the light, bending it into the empty space between sky and land.

I wish these pricks would leave us alone, Candy. You remember how we used to dare each other to jump up and down on the bridge, the way it rocked like a canoe tied to a dock? The closer the juniors got, the more it swayed. The more I wondered why you did it alone. It must have been quick, because the more I stood there, night after night, the more I wanted to live. For nothing more than to avoid the chill of the water on my skin. Wait till summer, I told myself.

•

"Is this the part where you beg me to repent," I said, "force me to confess, make me get down on my knees, and suck your dicks or the whole world will know how I pushed her off the bridge, watched her hit her head, refused to jump in after her?"

"I told you he was a psycho," letter jacket said, phone held out, no doubt recording everything. "Nobody gives a shit about us now. Touchdowns, Spell Bowl, breakups. You and Candy is all anyone ever talks about."

"You want a show," I said, taking off my jacket. Shotgun shells scattered across the warped wooden planks. I put my foot on the metal guardrail. I should be thinking about you, but I was imagining Leo DiCaprio as Romeo, the way he hit that water in the final scene, not even a flinch. I've watched it a hundred times since you jumped. The rewinding put me at ease. I hoped for a different ending.

"We know all about grief, Gavin," the one with glasses shouted. His arms came up hard from his hips, a basketball player making a difficult pass, the other three crowding in.

Stray hairs dashed across their chins, body spray reeking, threatening the copper smell of the river, the must of rotting trees.

I get my other foot up, my shoulders tipping forward, hips braced against the top of the rail, balanced. I was finally ready to jump. Those boys would be my witnesses. The water below was immune to everything above it.

They hesitated. None of them wanted to be the one to throw the punch that led to my drowning.

"Fuck your stories," I said. "None of us was good enough for her. And oh my god, did she know it. You, and you, and you. And me."

I didn't mean for it to go so far. You know my balance was shit. I couldn't even walk down the center of the road, my shoulder always nudging you farther and farther to the edge, your ankles irritated from the spray of rocks your feet kicked up.

The space between being poised on the edge and falling into the river was as fast as the flick of your mother's lighter. I didn't have time to close my eyes or my mouth before water was hissing past my ears, tightening around my neck, coldness blooming from my chest. I thought this would be the moment you'd find me, guide me to whatever happened next. But maybe I was disturbed too soon. Because in the confusion of their arms wrapping my waist, bodies twisting in retreat, the smell of synthetic leather as the sleeve of that letterman's jacket brushed across my face, us falling in a spasm of sodden clothes onto the muddy shore, you never appeared.

●

You hear stories like ours and people wonder how it could go so wrong. They make a big deal of our "suicide pact" as if people don't break promises all the time. I've tried not to use your death for personal gain. Every narration is an attempt at fame, at belonging, at getting other people to give a fuck. I go to the bar, and someone recognizes me. How, I'm not sure. Maybe I've got tragedy written all over my face. The women settle in close, their hips nestled against my leg, laughing wildly. The men stand, coiled, ready to call *bullshit* as if they'd believe the truth, as if they aren't a part of this spectacle themselves. I've tried to remove myself, but there are nights when being an adult is just too much strain on someone who was supposed to flash away at fifteen. You called me oblivious once, but your death was the rotten fruit of knowledge.

Here are the facts, I say, listing them: Candy jumped off a bridge. She likely broke her neck and drowned. I was her best friend. We made a pact. I'll never be the same.

Anything else is conjecture; estimates and guesses, like faulty wiring, spark sporadically. The pain is a dull but throbbing pulse connecting us like chemical bonds, elements weathering an invisible storm.

"Hey, sad man, tell us another," they say, lining up the shots in front of me, wagering when my words will slur too much for intelligibility.

"I knew a girl. Candy was her name. And I loved her."

This is where the story should stop. Or begin again and again.

Uncertain

1. We weren't supposed to be home, both of us feigning sick, underwear around our ankles. Senior year. Promises made to love each other forever.

2. Morning announcements interrupted by the turning on of TVs, the large boxes anchored to the walls, cobwebs sprayed across the backs like tinsel. September.

3. We had talked about baby names, imagining their personalities, a passing game that sounded like commitment. Eighteen years old, the pair of us.

4. Smoke billowed from the hole in the building. Teachers' faces crumpled with the immensity of the unknown. The silence a prowling hesitation.

5. I touched your hip, a new knowledge of heat.

6. The voices of news personalities bordering on hysterical, documenting history as it was unfolding. Accident, a fathomable explanation.

7. Promise, you asked, the angle of your eyes an invitation, a questioning of my sincerity I didn't comprehend.

8. The second plane, a ghostly shadow of the first. A mistaken replay. Teachers grasping for the remote, but clutching at their chests instead. The intake of breath just before the landing of a punch.

9. Jockeying for position, an awkwardness borne in inexperience. The meshing of two bodies beyond hugs and hand-holding. Anticipation.

10. Moments after, your head on my shoulder, the sheen of sweat drying, adhering body to body, thoughts spiraling like the fuselage of a plane toward an uncertain tragedy.

You've Stopped

You've stopped asking me to marry you. I think, finally, this is a good thing. "We're the last people on Earth," you cry into my ribs, your nose catching on each ridge of bone like a gate unlatching.

"We don't know that's true," I say, but the air in this bunker is getting heavy with our foul-smelling humidity. We're just springs rebounding and recoiling, thrusting our hands out in the dark, mauling the air, waiting to connect.

•

You've stopped gorging on Top Ramen and bubblegum. The floor is littered with wrappers, slick with noodles, and those little peas that cling to the bottom of my shoes. I keep the shoes on because I can't give up the idea of running, my calves refusing to forget, the muscles popping and stretching below me, warning of attrition.

"There's nowhere to run," I whisper, punching them twice a day, anyway.

"I do love you," you say, mistaking my regrets as compliments.

•

You've stopped checking the latch on the containment door. The fear of being invaded has become trampled dust, the network of shoe imprints you trace across the floor, pacing to keep the edge of possibility fresh in your mind. This you refuse to stop, coming closer and closer to my hip, my knees. Proximity, when we lived above, often created desire. But now you dart, zig, and zag like a goldfish in too small of a bowl. I miss your skin by millimeters.

•

You've stopped talking, your voice caking over with fallen dust motes because you declined to wear the hospital masks I had provided.

"Then how will we kiss?" you asked at my first suggestion.

Survival, at first, felt flirty, like finding ourselves alone in a hotel while everyone else was at the beach. Now, I'm pretty sure the beach doesn't exist. You still assume the world is out there, waiting for us, that we've merely stepped off the page of this fairytale you've been writing in your head.

•

You've stopped waking up unless prodded by my fingers checking your neck for a pulse. A bear in hibernation, eyelids crusted in allergy and lethargy. Even your heart has slowed. I whisper that I love you a hundred times a day, seizing on the lightning-bug blip of your heart as it pushes back against my palm, its own cadence letting me know that I'm too late.

Naming the Darkness

The night before Y2K, we set up the tent in the backyard. A skim of snow layered across hibernating grass, the temperatures promising to drop below freezing. We explained our need to be with the natural world without mentioning my brother's looming deployment. Never mind the buzzing of security lights from the trailer court that abutted our property line or the swish of cars drifting through our single-stoplight town. Our parents wanted us in church, hands growing hot from holding melting candles as the elders prayed and the congregation sang hymns. Leave us alone, we wanted to shout, but we knew that would only bring our parents closer. Space and privacy were conditional freedoms, especially for me at fourteen. I had started to notice our dad's subtle attempts at keeping us apart.

Our mother already in the van, our father stood near the door, arms crossed, head bowed as if he were too disappointed to look at us. "Your mother says I can't make you go. Says she won't hit you over the head with Christ's love."

"Hit with love? Is that what happened to you, Dad?" Dane said, just out of our father's reach.

I pulled the collar of my shirt over my nose to avoid the smell of seared steak, the earthy scent of mushrooms from that night's dinner.

Our father leaned toward us like a dog caught by the end of a heavy chain. "Whatever your plans are, make sure you're in the goddamn tent by the time we get home."

He closed the door on our smirks, our reflections in the leaded glass making us laugh. Church was something to avoid, a set of rules to ward off a death we never expected to experience. Even Y2K's promise of minor catastrophe was a joke that Dane and I passed back and forth like the chorus of a nursery rhyme.

For weeks, our parents forced us to carry in bottles of water and cheap ramen to the basement, stacking the packages next to jugs filled with gasoline settling on the mauve carpet. Dane lit matches, the flame flashing across his ochre eyes while he waved the matches around like sparklers, threatening to scar my skin. When the flame touched his fingertips, the blackened sulfurous heads disappearing into the deciduous weave of the carpet, I'd kick and kick while Dane laughed and expected he'd live forever.

For an hour we amused ourselves in the tent, sleeping bags pooling around our waists, while Dane sipped from a bottle of stolen Malibu, his lips becoming soft and purple, whispers crackling into shouted impersonations of our father. "By God, goddamn, God-given, godforsaken, god blast it," his voice arcing into sloppy edges like paint applied in wet, gelatinous strokes.

"Do you think Dad loves Him?"

"Who?"

"You know," I said, bringing my palms together.

"Seth, you look like a goddamn monk," Dane said. "Dad loves Mom. Period. Now drink this, or you'll be cold."

I wanted to love everyone, take them all into my heart, and put them to bed. Sarcasm was something I hadn't acquired yet, but Dane was a good example, and I was learning. I thought this would make me tougher, a wall against what I thought were our father's weaknesses. Our father was open to "The Mystery of Christ," but I needed something tangible, like Dane, who—though unpredictable and sometimes cruel—made my life more exciting.

I took a small sip, my lips already buzzing. "How can you drink this shit?"

"It ain't for pussies," he said, unzipping the tent. The cold lurched in like an animal escaping a cage.

"I'm not," I said, dropping into the folds of my sleeping bag.

Dane loomed over me, smiling, teeth exposed, eyes dulled marbles. "You're right, Seth. You ain't. A whole world full of 'em. But not you. Now get. Otherwise, we're going to miss it."

The plan was to climb the water tower. See for ourselves the moment of total darkness when all the computers glitched. Those numbers never rolling to 2000. For someone who still used a night light, it was hard to imagine. For Dane, it was just another challenge, a way to test his resolve, to name something he could do that our father and his teachers would never attempt. He saw himself as an adventurer without a map, scuttling behind parked cars, avoiding the violence that was promised to erupt.

We walked down the side streets, dipping into the shadows whenever we saw someone through a window—washing dishes, putting kids to bed, dancing in front of a drooping Christmas tree. If that were the adulthood waiting for me, I didn't want it.

We stopped in the parking lot of our parents' church, the back door glowing, welcoming. We both knew it was unlocked.

"You seen Ashley around?" I said.

"Let's just say she ain't praying for me anymore," Dane said, his voice brittle. He grabbed the back of my jacket, pulled me in close. "It's all bullshit, anyway."

I wasn't so sure, but at fourteen, I didn't feel I had the right to question his feelings. My questions often resulted in bruised arms from the erratic punches Dane threw when he was pissed at me. I see it now in a way I couldn't back then. He wanted someone, especially me, to just understand him. No questions asked.

Streetlights buzzed above us as we walked through the deserted streets, wind finding the hollows of our coats. The occasional car drifted toward us, engines hammering, brakes squeaking when the vehicles rolled through stop signs. Even on New Year's Eve, our town couldn't afford any police officers. As it neared midnight, there was no one to enforce the curfew.

We cut behind the one-story apartment buildings painted eggshell white and streaked with dust from the rusty train cars that rattled through town in the middle of the night. We ran past the grain elevator and up a frozen hill of oil-soaked soil dotted with years of unsold, spoiled corn kernels.

"I'm the king of the castle," I shouted.

Dane grabbed me by the arms and threatened to throw me off, but I broke at the knees, driving my shoulder into his ankles. He toppled and skidded down the hill. "You're getting faster," he said. "Meaner, too." His breath raced toward the sky, dissipating into the wink of faraway galaxies.

I stood above him, pulse thudding, thinking about all those times he'd pinned me to the ground, his body heavy against my arms, while I flailed, that fear of never getting up, of being at the complete mercy of the person holding you down. Dane would always wait until I cried, before grinding our foreheads together, a last shock of pain, then rolling away, laughing, daring me to come after him, so he could knock me down again.

Now, he pulled at the sleeve of his coat revealing a

Casio watch with glowing digital numbers. "Shit, we're going to miss it, Seth."

We ran across the tracks, around the bar lit up by fluorescent beer signs and a few security lights before drifting back into the shadows of the narrow side street lined by one-story houses, sentries guarding the entrance to the water tower. This wasn't a part of town that I was familiar with, so I was glad to have Dane, who was ready for anything, even in the cold.

Lights followed the bulbous curve of the tank, pooling under an eight-foot fence. Dane boosted me halfway up the fence, and I scrambled over the rest. The drop vibrated through my shoes as I waited for an alarm to go off. Dane landed beside me, feet already moving toward the solo ladder. He flashed me his watch.

"We've only got a few minutes to get to the top," he said, foot poised on the first step. There was something happy but determined about this pose. In the years after he was gone, this was how I liked to remember him. Young, capable, solid.

Each step we took, the ladder rattled, paint peeling off, looping toward the ground like bird feathers. I swallowed my questions, needing all my stray thoughts focused on the next rung. The tread of his boots, the melting snow, a wedged pebble, kept me steady as we raced up the twelve stories. If our father was praying, I hoped it was for our safety. Suspended halfway above the ground and the catwalk surrounding the water tower, I wanted to believe that there was something powerful enough to protect me if I fell.

At the top, Dane helped me fit my feet into the narrow groove of the catwalk. As we tried to reel our breaths back into our aching lungs, the aircraft warning lights strobed the side of Dane's face. He reached for my shoulder, and I flinched at his image; he looked like one of those horror-movie villains pulling a victim toward a flashing blade. He caught me as I wobbled.

"Jesus, Seth, let's keep the tragedy to a minimum, yeah?"

"How much time's left?" I gripped the railing, the cold biting into my uncovered palms, but I refused to let go. The town below was lit in uneven strands of light, most of the streets submerged in darkness. It reminded me of the yearly planetarium visit. The way the presenter connected the dots between stars, taking for granted that we shared his vision. I never could see the patterns. Everything looked like happenstance to me. Like most events during those years, it wasn't as impressive as I'd hoped, and regret seeped in. The thought of climbing down the ladder backward was worse than the cold.

"Thirty seconds," he said. "Fucking town is depressing. I don't know if I can live here another minute."

"How do you know someplace else is better?"

"Because any place is better than here," Dane said.

He said things and expected me to swallow it like pure oxygen. I wanted to chew on it, digest what I could, but he was always so quick to get moving again. "Even if you might get killed?"

"We're all going to die, Seth. How's that for a prophecy? You saw them people dancing in front of that Christmas tree. Saw how fucking sad it was? I ain't holding on to nothing," Dane said, leaning out over the railing.

Don't fall, don't fall, I thought, but I had an image of that guy in that *Titanic* movie, screaming into the rushing wind of that ship, how he didn't know nothing about the death that was coming for him.

We didn't hold hands or count down. I thought maybe we'd pray, but we huddled together, the sounds of semis air-braking as they came upon the stoplight just outside the town line, a few miles to the west. The Casio faithfully ticked down the seconds until the digits changed to twelve-zero-zero.

Nothing changed below. I rubbed at my eyes, but the lights didn't even flicker. I shuffled my feet to get some warmth back into my toes. The catwalk trembled alive, threatening to throw us from its back. A car alarm went off near the bar.

"He couldn't even get this right?" Dane grabbed me by the shoulders, that red light pulsing across his eye, his breath snorting out like a bull's.

"Well, it's a miracle, of course," I said, already apologizing to God, asking for safe travels down the ladder.

"We're all fools. Thinking it would just end."

"Hallelujah!" I shouted. I hoped it would reach Mom and Dad. Ashamed I had doubted them.

In answer, the church bells rang.

"Come on, Dane," I said, but he stood there, arms braced against the railing. I was shivering. "Let's go celebrate with Mom and Dad."

"You think anyone down there gives a fuck about me?" His elbow sliced through the air connecting with the metal of the tower tank. A dull thud came in response. I know he wanted it to be louder, but he just didn't have enough force. None of us did. I was newly realizing that some things were unmovable.

"I just want to go home, Dane. You promised we'd make it back to the tent in time." The lights were still there, but so was the cold, and the happiness I had felt was fading.

"Why don't you pray about it, Seth? All your other prayers have been answered, right?"

"Why can't you believe? In something?"

Before Dane could answer, I was pounding down the ladder, my fingers so cold they didn't want to bend around the steps. I had that feeling of something watching me, but every time I looked over my shoulder, I was submerged in light, a gentle hand guiding me down toward the relative safety of the ground. This was better than the baptism I'd received at the church earlier in the year. The water had been fierce with desire to enter my body, the rush of darkness squeezing my chest, and then I was ripped back into consciousness, applause echoing until the water seeped from my ears.

At the bottom of the ladder, I tried to scale the fence by myself, but it was too high.

When Dane finally stepped onto the ground behind me, he said, "Running out of miracles?"

"Fuck you," I said, but it was softer than a pulled punch.

"People. That's all there is. Me, and you, and Dad. Billions of us. Laughing and crying and fucking each other over. Handing out a boost occasionally. You'll see."

He helped me scrabble over the fence, and I ran. He'd either come with me or he wouldn't. I didn't have time to look back anymore.

We ran back through town, Dane passing me easily, my lungs constricting like a popped balloon. He cheered me on in a hushed voice, porch lights blurring. *You'll make a good soldier*, I wanted to tell him.

But he stopped in the back lot of our parents' church, that light still shining through its unlocked door. He bent over, hands on his knees, waiting for me.

"What are you doing? Come on, we're almost there," I said, putting my arm around his shoulder. We stood there for a minute, spots before my eyes. I still hoped we could sneak back into the tent.

"Gotta do something," he said, walking stiffly toward the door. "Help me."

I don't want to say this was the moment I made a decision, because I can't remember pausing, thinking anything, really. Dane would call it all bullshit, anyway, but I followed him into that church, the light guiding us down the hallway back into the shadows until we entered the sanctuary. It was quiet except for our ragged breathing. Heat surrounded us from bodies that had just left, a thickness that was hard to walk through. Dane shrugged off his coat and kneeled next to the podium, paintings of Jesus' trials of violence hanging above our heads, the blood like black ink in the darkness.

"What do I say?" he asked.

"You should ask for forgiveness. For faith. For light." I knelt beside him, holding my hands out in front of me the way Dad had taught us, trying to quiet my heart. I was still waiting for the world to break.

"Forgiveness for what? I just want to know where I'm going when I die. You've probably got years to figure this out. Where I'm going, there's a chance of dying every day."

"Maybe there won't be any wars for a while," I said.

"So there's no war right now. Soldiers get killed during basic, riding in helicopters, crossing the fucking street. Even Dad said I wouldn't make it. I heard him talking to Mom, her telling him to shut up, that she couldn't take it. So you tell me what I have to do, because praying ain't doing shit right now."

"Can I tell you a secret?" A passing car's lights washed across the wall, highlighting Jesus' eye, the crown of thorns, the gloss of blood. "Most of the time, while everyone is praying, I can only think of one word. I just think *Hallelujah* for as long as I can."

"Christ, Seth, you better hope you live to a hundred." Dane stood, dipped his head toward both paintings and then headed out the door.

I kneeled there for another second, happy, but confused, hoping I had said the right thing.

Leaving the church and entering the cold again was like

stepping out of a hot shower. I felt sluggish, the kind of tired where you'd lie down just about anywhere. Dane dragged me along that last half-mile, guiding us through the trailer court around cracked driveways and flimsy-curtained windows to our backyard. The tent sat upright, darkened, but zipped against animal intruders. The car sat in the driveway, engine still pinging from working so hard in the cold. The house was dark, quiet, and closed-off. Dane tried the handle, but the door was locked.

"Shit. I guess ol' Dad won this one. One less night listening to him snoring."

I wasn't looking forward to sleeping in the cold, but another night near Dane was a good trade. I meant to take time more seriously. To care a little more about the people around me.

Once we were inside the tent, Dane fit the sleeping bag over my legs and chest. I shivered violently. Dane tucked himself into his own sleeping bag and waddled closer, almost tripping over my feet. Awkwardly, he lay next to me, the fabric swishing like the hiss of a sparkler thrown into a bucket of water.

"Those lights," he said, his mouth close to my ear, a warm current in the middle of a lake. "They're fucking constant. Steady, you know? Like me, Seth. I'm unwavering."

I wanted to take something from him, hold the gun, the grenade, a tourniquet if necessary, but none of this was available yet. Until Dane left, I was supposed to act like the usual younger brother. I was the one who was supposed to be held, prodded, protected. Something was coming for him, even then, I could feel it, but I was helpless to stop it. Our father thought we were held in the palm of a merciful God, that we were too small to change the course of this predestination, so he prayed in the dark.

"Hallelujah," I said, lips so close to Dane's cheek, they could barely open.

About the Author

Tommy Dean is the author of two flash-fiction chapbooks, *Special Like the People on TV* (Redbird Chapbooks, 2014) and *Covenants* (ELJ Editions, 2021). He lives in Indiana, where he is currently the editor at *Fractured Lit* and *Uncharted Magazine*. A graduate of the Queens University of Charlotte MFA program, he is currently working on a novel. A recipient of the 2019 Lascaux Prize in Short Fiction, his writing can be found in *Best Microfiction 2019* and *2020*, *Best Small Fictions 2019*, *Monkeybicycle*, and *Atticus Review*. He taught writing workshops for the Gotham Writers Workshop, the Barrelhouse Conversations and Connections conference, and the Lafayette Writers Workshop. Find him at tommydeanwriter.com and on Twitter at @TommyDeanWriter.

Author

Acknowledgments

You're never quite sure you're writing a story collection until it's done. Ten years of starts and stops, flourishes, and frustration have led to this book in your hands, so thank you for being a generous reader.

My family, Shelby, Alayna, and Pacey are a constant fountain of support and inspiration. Our own fine-arts school in action! There are no words, no revisions, no time spent alone without the support and encouragement from my wife! We've always been a team!

All of my fiction has been inspired or touched by my family. Thank you for loving me for me!

A huge lifetime thank you to Leah Angstman for her drive to create the fantastic Alternating Current Press. A place I'm thrilled to call home! Leah made every part of this book better. A super-talented editor and publisher, who somehow does it all!

Thank you to the editors and readers of the literary magazines in which these stories first appeared. You saw something in these stories first, and I'm grateful for your time and talents!

My reading teams at *Fractured* and *Uncharted*, thank you for your constant inspiration, your love for flash and genre fiction, your love for the art of stories! The editors of the sister sites, thank you for your constant support! You're doing the work! Special thanks to Josh Roark for giving me the opportunity to live my dream job! Inspiration begets inspiration. And to Scott Segal for the vision and the trust! Everyone at DNA has a special place in my heart!

All the gratitude to Kathy, Fish, Andrew Porter, and Susan Perabo who found merit and light and hope, and something stirring in these stories, in this book, whose words will carry me beyond this book and onto the blank page of the next one!

Beta readers extraordinaire! You made these stories infinitely better and gave me the confidence to send them out into the world! Thank you, Cathy Ulrich, Kristin Tenor, Amy Barnes, Brianne Kohl, Hannah Grieco, Jennifer Fliss, Megan Neville, Maura Yzmore, Janice Leagra, Josh Denslow, Gaynor Jones, Ami Hendrickson, Maureen Langloss, Joshua Jones, Kathryn McMahon, Kate Finegan, T. L. Sherwood, and many more wonderful writers and friends!

My Twitter writing community who helped me find a writing home, a place to share success and disappointments, a place to feel like a writer, a place to find ways to explore writing craft and the ups and downs of this vocation. Special thank you to the Flash Avengers who have made my writing life and my real life so much better through their generosity and kindness, as well as through their inspiring talent. I'm a better writer and person for knowing each one of you! I wish everyone this type of writing community!

It's been 12 years since I graduated from my Queens University of Charlotte MFA program, but a special thanks to my professors who first championed my early writing. Thank you for providing not only craft knowledge, but the inspiration to keep writing! Thank you, Fred Leebron, Michael Kobre, Elissa Schapell, and Naeem Murr. Special thanks to Lauren Groff and Elizabeth Strout for their patience and guidance, and friendship. You made me believe even in those moments I wanted to give up.

I've made some special friendships through this writing journey. There's no book without Tara Stillions Whitehead, Janice Leagra, Kathy Fish, Meg Pokrass, Kim Magowan, Davon Loeb, Dan Crawley, K. B. Carle, Barlow Adams, Melissa Ostrom, Cathy Ulrich, Jackie Doyle, Jolene Mcllwain, Maureen Langloss, Tara Isabel Zambrano, K. C. Mead-Brewer, Sara Freligh, Francine Witte, Jad Josey, Amy Barnes, Meg Pillow, Cassie Mannes Murray, April Bradley, Julia Fierro, Andria Williams, Tara Laskowski, Cheryl Pappas, and so many more!

And because I don't know when the next book will come out, thank you to all of the people who have supported my journey as a writer. Writing is a solitary and often lonely venture, but the people I have met and will meet in the future are the little solar lights dotted along the way.

Previous Publications

"Here" and "Carrying the Weight" were previously published in *New World Writing*.

"Hollows" was previously published in *The Lascaux Review*.

"Always the Alpha" was previously published in *Bull: Men's Fiction* and *The Strand Magazine*.

"A Thrumming Silence" and "Ruthlessly, Denying" were previously published in *JMWW*.

"Wave" and "Finding Fame on Cautionary Billboards" were previously published in *The Journal of Compressed Creative Arts*.

"Rock, Paper, Scissors" was previously published in *Vestal Review*.

"A Small Act of Contrition" was previously published in *The MacGuffin*.

"God's Eye" was previously published in *Split Lip Magazine*.

"Without Permission" was previously published in *Spry Literary Journal*.

"When the Waters Came" was previously published in *Cotton Xenomorph*.

"Three Boys in the Woods" was previously published in *(b)OINK*.

"We're Trying to Tell You" was previously published in *Bull: Men's Fiction*.

"Arriving" and "Filaments of Air" were previously published in *r.kv.r.y.*

"Just the Father" was previously published in *The Avalon Literary Review*.

"Baby, Alone" was previously published in *Watershed Review*.

"The Age of Quitters" was previously published in *2 Bridges Review*.

"Airbrushed" was previously published in *Newfound*.

"When Mono Was Part of the Equation" was previously published in *Longleaf Review*.

"Open to an Ocean" was previously published in *X-Ray Literary Magazine*.

"Stitches Unraveling" was previously published in *New Flash Fiction Review*.

"Knocking" was previously published in *Pithead Chapel*.

"Covenants" was previously published in *The Citron Review*.

"If It Weren't for the Lights" was previously published in *Claw & Blossom*.

"Candy: A Teenage Gospel" was previously published in *Lost Balloon*, *The Lascaux Review*, and *After the Pause*.

"You've Stopped" was previously published in *Pithead Chapel*, *Best Microfiction 2019*, and *Best Small Fictions 2019*.

Colophon

The edition you are holding is the First Edition of this publication.

The titles are set in Landsdowne, created by Paul Lloyd. The wide sans-serif font is set in Alcubierre, created by Matt Ellis. The narrow sans-serif font is set in Avenir Book, created by Adrian Frutiger. The Alternating Current Press logo is set in Portmanteau, created by JLH Fonts. All other text is set in Iowan Old Style, created by John Downer. All fonts used with permission; all rights reserved.

Cover designed by Leah Angstman, with image by Felix Mittermeier. The Alternating Current lightbulb logo created by Leah Angstman, ©2013, 2022 Alternating Current. Author photo taken by ©Jamie Johnson at Signature Studio. All images used with permission; all rights reserved.

Other Works from
Alternating Current Press

All of these books (and more) are available at
Alternating Current's website: press.alternatingcurrentarts.com.

alternatingcurrentarts.com

Made in United States
Orlando, FL
15 July 2022

19744875R00098